WHERE GOD WON'T REMEMBER

A story by Shawny Fin

For Billy....

I miss you every day, dad.

1874.

He couldn't see the cold of his breath, but he knew in the dark it was there. He couldn't feel his fingers or toes due to the midnight cold of winter in Boston, but he knew they were still there. The deep ache of his body caused him to shift, and still, the iron collar about his throat was there. The chain anchoring him to the stone wall did not jangle like a steel chain, but had a dullness to its sound, like that of thick lead. Its weight long ago dragged him down to live on the damp floor.

The sound of pounding boots coming toward his cell not only tensed up his body, but his spirit as well – and how they both called out for relief. To be free. And in the endless darkness of prison the only freedom one could dare hope for was the freedom offered in dying.

He could tell by the sound of the hard heels that there would be three of them tonight.

The clang of keys and the turning of the lock tore from him a shudder for the whipping to come…

He snapped awake from the nightmare in a bolt, gulping for breath, his hand subconsciously going to the gun on his hip. He drew in a hard breath at last, over the pounding in his chest.

He was no longer in his cell. It had been many years since he was released from Fort Warren prison. Well over a decade. Most days though, he felt he traded one cell for another – released from the cold dark, and unleashed into the hell of battle.

He went to the inside pocket of his vest and pulled out his last cigarette, before his mind wandered into the memories of the war.

After placing the cigarette in the corner of his mouth he pat himself down for a fusee, and found he didn't have one.

A gentleman ahead began a coughing fit that ended with him doubled over and gasping for air. Clearly the man had some form of lung trouble.

After a heavy sigh, he returned the cigarette to his inside pocket anyway. And there he also felt the wad of cash he won two nights ago. The wad of cash and who he crossed to win it were his reason for leaving.

Leaving on the last train before midnight and heading toward the northern frontier. He had his fill of Chicago. And in his way, Chicago had enough of him.

This last poker game – his primary income of the last many years of drifting should the random farm not require any hand work– had been with wanted men, whom he believed were looking for him to settle the matter of him being accused of cheating the game.

Which he did.

Seven hundred dollars was nothing at which he should sneeze, he knew. He could live on that amount for a year if he really needed to – he had been through worse years. He knew hunger and filth well since the war. Especially filth on his hands.

The kind of filth that may never wash off.

The train was still in the station, not yet on their way northwest. It was almost midnight he figured.

He resettled back into his seat and put his gaze out the window.

Where had the years gone?

The farm, the war and all the years drifting across the country since. And still he was only thirty-four years old. Thirty-four, but he looked well into his forties. The wear of a man who had seen his share of brutality and the darkest side of mankind. He had survived many things to be troubled as he was.

The drifter thought all of this as he readjusted himself in the seat again. He didn't carry much but a knapsack and his hat. And the knapsack didn't have much in it but a few necessities for his gun, a small blanket and a couple of pears to hold him off until the train ride was over. He always traveled light in these times.

The times of looking over his shoulder.

The steam whistle blared and the engine tied itself on giving the entire chain of four cars a modest shove. This train would ride the rails all through the night to the end of the line, delivering mail and newspapers that's ink was still wet.

And that was exactly where the drifter wanted to go.

Always as far away as possible. Always on the move.

"Move fast, move quiet," he whisperer to himself. The memory of his young friend, a native Arapaho scout named Singing Quiet. A brave man who often said this quote on their many deep wilderness treks for elk or bear or what the Federal government called renegades. Singing Quiet earned his name because of his lack to open his mouth when he sang – he only hummed.

He reached up and touched a thin scar in the side of his neck, an arrow slice given to him by Singing Quiet the day they met.

The drifter smiled at the memory.

The longest he ever stayed anywhere since the war ended however was here in Chicago. Six long months. Working and saving money for the winter. He would never sleep on a cold damp floor again, he swore to himself when he was released to fight for the Union.

The nightmares never went away but they had faded some over the years. Those terrors of the 15 months of his imprisonment. The incident in Middle Park when he was assigned to Saint Vrains – which led to his incarceration and later returned into Army service to fight in Tennessee…

And just then it occurred to him it was the first time he thought of Singing Quiet and didn't think of how the man died.

He sighed heavily to himself, watching the various people bustling to catch the train out of Chicago that night. There was a couple kissing goodbye, standing in the midst of fanciful luggage, being loaded by two porters. The woman held a ticket in her hand. He couldn't read the ticket from his seat, but by her dress he guessed she was bound for St. Paul, or even Minneapolis, their new neighbor. Neither were far enough for the drifter. Neither were the end of the line.

As he watched the couple, for a moment he allowed himself to wonder how different his life would have been, had he taken a wife and stayed on the farm, the life his mother wanted for him. He watched how deeply the couple loved each other, desperate to not be apart, but driven apart, no doubt by desperation in such times. Their eyes were locked together as if they were sewn in such a way by God.

Was she going home? Or was she going on ahead to make a new one?

Home. The idea of home had terrified him at times. Returning home and taking all of these demons with him. It gave him a sense of shame, despite his intentions always being in the right place. It took a massacre, prison and a war to turn him into a drifting card cheat.

A man with no purpose but to exist – to barely survive. He didn't know if that made him more dangerous or no threat at all.

The woman came through the door then and the drifter nodded politely to her and she smiled with only half of her mouth – he could see she had been crying. He helped her with her bag, stowing it overhead as she took her seat. She thanked him, but he said nothing in return.

Just after her six men boarded loudly as he fell back into his seat across from the woman. Dock workers, he could tell, most likely straight from a saloon. No doubt wanting to tie on a good drunk so to sleep the entire way to wherever it was they were going. Their noses were ruddy, and they spoke at a volume entirely unnecessary for a quiet passenger car. The woman sighed to herself in a way that rolled her eyes.

Irish.

He smirked at her detestment toward the race of Erin. And yet also noticed she was too well-natured to address the men's behavior.

The drifter agreed with her, but at the same time understood the disposition of hard-working men. He was raised on a farm, after all, and had at one time been a foreigner himself – before Mexico had been made into California when he was a small boy.

The last of them jammed his bag into the rack above the drifter and plopped himself down in the seat ahead of him. The mans breathing and mAnnerisms loud and obnoxious as he got settled in.

The loud man turned around and held out his hand, "Name's Joseph Cullen," he said. His thick Irish accent almost impossible to understand. And the slack of his jaw loaded with tobacco couldn't help but make this man all the more Annoying. Not that the drifter personally didn't like the Irish, in the army his first sergeant was an Irishman, a man named Sullivan, who was quite firm but fair. But the Irish had a disposition for excessive celebration, and a reputed deafness for those whom it bothered. And all the drifter wanted was quiet. To slip out of the city, never to return.

The drifter starred at him for a short moment and eventually held out his hand.

"Jonah."

"Pleased to meet ya, Jonah lad," he said, roughly clapping hands with him. "Where ya headed?"

The man's volume was already Annoying to Jonah, the drifter. The man was loud, and Jonah didn't like loud – not in the darker hours of the night with a long train ride ahead of them. He had experienced enough loud in his days to last several lifetimes.

"End of the line."

"No lyin'?" Cullen said, pulling back in his seat to exaggerate his surprise. "Us too. We work for the Western Union Telegraph Company now – the only work available who's hirin' Irish and on the frontier to boot. We're headin' into, uhh… Minnesota! To set up the cable in this lumber town…Oy, Oisin! What's the name of that little town were goin' to?"

"New Arbor!" Jonah heard from the back. Another Irish accent. The drifter groaned in his mind – his destination as well. He tried recalling again just then how long the train would take to reach the destination, and how long he would have to tolerate this Cullen before he passed out.

Not soon enough.

"Aye, New Arbor. Where all the whores are blonde with blue eyes and speak three words of English. And rumor has it that the Western Union is goin' to buy that lumber company and set up poles all the way across the Dakota Nation to California. So do you work for Western-"

"Lookit, I'd rather travel with just my thoughts, Cullen," he interupted.

And with that the drifter calmly lowered his head and put his hat over his eyes, saying not another word. He could smell the reek of booze on the Irishman and didn't really see an end to this pointless conversation anytime soon. A conversation he has heard countless times. There was a brief silence while Jonah let him think about what to do next.

He heard Cullen stand and walk away, tugging his bag down from the rack. He mumbled something as he stomped off toward the back and the rest of his group, but the drifter took not enough attention to calculate it for actual language. The man Cullen no doubt reverting to his native tongue to cuss away at Jonah's rudeness.

But it was the only true language men like that spoke. Assertiveness – which ironically he also learned from Sullivan, his first army sergeant.

The drifter couldn't help but allow the smallest of smiles under his hat as his attention was quiet again.

"Good for you, sir," the woman whispered from the corner of her mouth to the drifter. Though her eyes stayed forward.

Windfalls of levity were rare to him, but when they happened, he embraced it. And if he was being honest with himself they made him forget all the terrible occurrences since leaving the farm in '60. Again he thought of home for a moment and had been compelled to do so more often over the last few months. Was it time? Was mother still alive? He had a sister too – Mother…Luna Isabella, whom his father called his Moon Queen. He began letters many years ago and had written many since, but he never sent them. He didn't know how to explain the things he had seen, or justify them to people who couldn't have been there.

He wasn't sure if his imprisonment was communicated to his family by the army – he suspected not, having heard no word from home in his time there. Or no word that was allowed to reach him, anyway.

How was he suppose to explain to his mother or sister how he was changed since those years ago. When a young man full of destiny rode away from the farm to join the army and do his part for the country.

His mother didn't agree with his decision, but she respected it. His father had passed a few years earlier. His grandfather wholeheartedly disagreed and forbid him to go, but what twenty years old with a made up mind could hear him?

But in the last year or so he seemed to be taking on less weight in the shoulders. Was it time? Would it ever be time? A part of him was waiting to die. Waiting for a grave, caught cheating at poker or just being in the wrong place at the wrong time as he roamed around the country.

Two nights earlier, at the small back-alley grogshop called Red Gretchen's, he was at the tail end of a fourteen-hour poker game. It was down to him, and a mouthy young runt named Pete Vogal, who kept attesting that he killed six men. He knew Vogal was wanted, but for murder? Jonah wasn't so sure.

Every time Vogal made this claim, his friends and the larger-than-normal crowd that night would laugh at him. Pete was the jittery type, even when exhausted and drunk. He had a scar that took his right eye, leaving it a milky white – Pete being too young to have gotten such a token in the war. Perhaps he thought that would have intimidated Jonah, but nothing of the sort could do such. Jonah had seen boys younger than Pete have their foot sawed off in an army hospital tent and make barely a whimper. He had seen men meet their violent and bloody death without shedding a tear, fearlessly and proudly meeting God at the speed of cAnnon fire.

Eventually the long game came down to it, and they were both all-in. Jonah called, and Pete laid down a full house.

While his friends went wild, Pete leaned back in his chair with a nasty smirk on his face, his one good eye bloodshot from whisky, his face a dead and confident calm. It was the first time the boy closed his mouth the entire game.

The drifter sighed, looking down at his cards.

"What you got, Jonah, you lanky, unfed, som'bitch?" Pete said, sure of himself that he had finally beaten the drifter. And truly a full house is a strong hand, especially when the game is down to only two players.

Jonah looked at Pete, and around at Pete's friends. There were about seven of them, all together, and half the room who wanted to see the drifter lose after all this time. Jonah quietly laid down his cards so that everyone could read them.

Four eights.

The Pete crowd's demeanor went from that of a wedding to a funeral.

Jonah had won.

Pete flew up and out of his chair and his hand went for his pistol, but three of his friends grabbed him before it went off, knowing better and being less emotionally drunk. Pete screaming about being cheated. Pete knew Jonah was cheating, but he was cheating too.

One of Pete's companions, a very tall man, though young, in a black hat looked at the drifter and said, "Don't you think you better get the hell out of here, mister?" His tone told Jonah that he was not really asking. And the palm resting on his gun gave the drifter all the assurance he needed that this man was aware of all the facts – both men had cheated, but Jonah was just better at it.

The drifter looked around the saloon and he wondered if he was getting back to his hotel across town in one piece.

Jonah the drifter had just won near a thousand dollars.

He scrapped his winning chips into his hat. He walked up to Gretchen, who tended her own bar, the ragged old whore she was, and said loud enough for all to hear "Drinks are on me!"

The woman, who held the game cash, handed him his winnings minus fifty dollars to cover the drinks.

The crowd was alive again at the call of free whisky!

The aggravated Pete flew again into a rage, his friends, still requiring three of them, holding him down. They kept whispering in his ear and harshly, trying calm him down

And as the crowd rushed the bar, Jonah vanished into the night. As he made the first turn down the alley, he could still hear Pete Vogal cursing him.

"God damn you Jonah, you better look over your shoulder 'til the day you die!"

It made him laugh to himself.

Jonah smiled recalling his escape from Red Gretchen's. And doing so, peeked out from under his hat, instinctively scanning the train station crowd one more time – wondering if Pete Vogal had tracked him down. But if Jonah was good at anything, it was disappearing when he wanted to. A talent he learned from Singing Quiet and his elders.

So it was time to move on from Chicago, and that is exactly what he was doing.

Always on the move.

The train shoved again and began to pull out of the station. Jonah put a hand to the inner pockets of his vest and felt the wad of bills there. After his train ticket, new fixings for his pistol, a new set of clothes, boots and a hat and treating himself to a bath and laundry, he had roughly seven hundred dollars left.

Plenty of paper for a fresh start. He could live a long time on seven hundred in cash and he meant to do so quietly in Minnesota since the train didn't go beyond that just now. A quiet winter on the edge of civilization amongst the Swedes and Norwegians.

Jonah adjusted in his seat a last time to settle back into a sleeping position.

He smiled at the irony of the Red Gretchen's situation. That the only person in play to see that he actually was cheating that night at was a one-eyed blowhard. And Vogal was good at it himself. After all, he made it to the last hand as well without being spotted and caught. The drifter chuckled then, guessing again how Pete Vogal lost that eye.

He enjoyed cards and knew it to be a reliable source of income from time to time, but also the dangers of cheating for a living. He learned to cheat in the Army. The Army before prison and the war.

The drifter took in a deep breath and let it out slowly. The gentle bucking of the train helped him wade off into a comfortable sleep – this one dreamless, just how he liked it.

A hard brake and the long blare of the train steam whistle woke Jonah from a dead sleep. Elevated voices.

The train was coming to a grinding halt.

Out the window was only the pitch black of night, he had no idea how long he had been asleep. The Irish line workers were up now and mumbling in confusion as well were the other few passengers.

Several of the rack lamps were still lit, so Jonah could see around the inside of the car.

The woman in the fanciful dress holding a hand over her chest in exasperation, a look of terror on her face. She looked to the drifter and asked, "My God, what did they say?"

Jonah could only respond with a confused look. He sat up slowly and peered out the window, but all that came back was his own reflection. He turned to the woman and asked if they already passed St. Paul and she nodded and said that there were no tickets sold for St. Paul so the train kept going.

That's when the gun fire erupted in the forward cars.

The woman gasped and the Irish workers began to murmur in their own tongue. Hysterics were taking over. Jonah was calm. The calmest of them all. And he did indeed have a pistol hanging on his hip, but he wondered if that was a wise move now. He felt the cash in his vest pockets again and wondered if he should try and stash it.

The woman squeaked and pointed out the window. A man on a horse carrying a torch went galloping passed the drifter's window.

Then another.

Too late, Jonah thought to himself, as he heard their boots pounding up the stairs and onto the decking of the train car.

The door was kicked open and the two men, both wearing bandanas over their faces, entered brandishing pistols, and each carrying a satchel.

"Ladies and gentlemen!" the taller of the two shouted. The entire population of the car fell silent. "You are being robbed. We had a couple heroes in the front cars and those heroes are dead. Hand out your cash and jewelry quick…" But he was interrupted by more gunfire exchanging in the forward cars. The taller man decided against pleasantries and went to work screaming at them for their money and putting his gun barrel in their face.

Jonah was about halfway down the car, and it was his turn. The smaller of the men approached and when he stood over the drifter, he could see that behind his bandana mask the robber's right eye was torn away with scarring, leaving it a dead milky white.

Pete Vogal.

Jonah's heart dropped in his chest, "Ah shit."

"*YOU!*" Pete said, recognizing him. Jonah had hoped that Pete was too drunk that night to remember anything, but apparently Jonah had made more of an everlasting impression than he realized. Pete put the barrel of his gun right to the drifter's forehead and pressed hard.

"What you got over there?" the other robber asked. Jonah knew then it was the same tall man who had told him to leave Gretchen's. His name was Gavin, if Jonah recalled hearing it right that night.

"I got that son of bitch that cheated me outta a thousand dollars." Pete said, pressing hard enough to leave a mark on Jonah's skin. The Irish workers and other passengers held frozen in their seats, their hands held up and shaking.

Jonah just stared back at him, facing his death. Death that he knew he deserved and had avoided countless times in his life. He wasn't about to give this wet-nosed runt the satisfaction of begging for his life.

"Just get his money and let's go, already." Gavin said. Jonah could hear in his voice that he was nervous and anxious to leave. Most likely his first robbery.

Pete and Jonah shared a moment then, staring each other down. Three unblinking eyes caught in a stoppage of time. Jonah had known many men who have taken lives for their country, and even in such situations it left a glimmer in the man's eye that never left him for all his days. He could see no such glimmer in the remaining eye of Pete Vogal. And Jonah, after staring him down hard gave a "huh," and leaned back slowly in his seat, coming away from the barrel, confident Pete Vogal had never killed anyone – or anything.

Jonah knew it. And he knew Pete knew it.

The drifter wouldn't blink. The woman across from him whimpered, certain this man was about to be shot dead where he sat.

Seeing that Pete was on the brink of explosion, Gavin pushed toward them both and as he passed the sitting Jonah, he used the butt of his pistol to sap the drifter's skull.

Blood and light exploded for the drifter, and in his stunned state he felt one of them ripping through his pockets and taking his cash.

"Quit fuckin' around, you got your money. Stick to the plan and let's go!" he heard Gavin say.

Jonah heard the woman in the fancy dress crying as Pete ripped her jewelry away, but by then his world was spinning. Jonah made an effort to get to his feet, but he fell forward. The last thing he heard was the woman crying about her red garnet wedding ring.

After that, he knew only darkness.

The throbbing in his head was ineffable. The woman whimpering. It was still dark outside his window, but all other noise, the noise of gunfire and robbers, had gone.

Head still a spinning top, Jonah tried to grab at anything to steady himself, but again went limp, collapsing face down.

After another undetermined amount of time, an explosion shook him from his daze, his body and mind recalling the artillery fire from years ago.

He groaned and lifted himself up, his mind was beginning to clear – Gavin had blasted him good. He knew his money was gone but decided to pat himself down anyway. Blood was matting the back of his hair.

They didn't take Jonah's gun.

The bandits probably didn't take his gun because it was an old Colt Dragoon. An outdated pistol, Jonah knew, but it served him well. The days were quickly fading away when old army veterans like Jonah used ball rounds. He was a dying breed, it seemed. But he didn't care. The younger generation preferred bullets and that was fine by him.

He gained his focus and looked around the passenger car. The woman in the dress crying her eyes out, robbed of all her decorations. What a night she was having, Jonah thought to himself.

Jonah grabbed his knapsack and refit his hat on his head, which made him wince for a moment.

"Which way?" he said to the crying lady.

She looked up at him through her soaked eyes in confusion. He could see her hysterical state of mind left her useless to him. He had seen it before, a terror in the face of death that locks up the mind.

Jonah knelt down in front of her and gently took her hand, for this was no battlefield, and she was no soldier.

"Ma'am," he began, "Those men are gone, and they took our possessions. I want justice done and to see our things returned. Thanks be to God that's all they took." And with that he covered her exposed breast with the ripped part of her dress where her silver necklace had been torn away.

The woman took a deep and stuttering breath, and she lifted a shaking finger and pointed out his window.

"They took off in that direction. Not a minute before you came to."

Jonah looked over his shoulder and then back to the woman.

"Go get 'em."

The drifter winked and stood back to his feet.

He didn't even bother using the door. He slid open his window and vaulted out to land lightly on the ground. He had to steady himself for a heartbeat once landed, but his bearings were coming back to him better by the minute. He looked up the length of the train, and along the way he saw many men holding lanterns and torches. These weren't the robbers though, he knew.

Aligned on the ground were three bodies of men, they all had bowler hats laid on their chests. And standing over them, dressed neatly and wearing bowler hats, were two other men and a woman, each with a silvery pistol on their hip. As they turned and spoke, Jonah caught a glimpse that they were also wearing badges.

How did the law get here so fast? How long was I out? Jonah thought to himself.

And then he remembered who wore the bowler hats and the shield badges because he had a run in with them a few months earlier.

"Pinkertons," Jonah whispered to himself. What the hell were they doing here? They were hired for investigations and protections. He wondered what, or who, else was aboard the train with him. What was it they were supposed to be protecting? Jonah shook the thought from his aching head. He could see that the engine was disabled, by the great plume of steam and shattered connecting rod – did he recall a dynamite blast while unconscious? Is that what woke him from his knock out? He shrugged the questions away and focused.

This train wasn't moving anytime soon. Nor were any to pass anytime soon back toward St. Paul.

He could hear the captain of the Pinkertons shouting orders to ride back to town and send a wire to the Marshall. Jonah didn't want to wait around for him either. And Jonah didn't know how far back town was. It felt like he could've been asleep for several hours, but he wasn't sure.

Jonah the drifter wanted his money back.

As quietly as he could, and without being seen, Jonah cut over into the tree line and disappeared into the woods. It was a moonless night. He went in about a half mile leaving the great hiss of the crippled train engine and murmuring of the Pinkerton's far behind him. And though it was nearly pitch black, he was able to make his way easily enough. He found himself an oak tree and sat against it. He didn't want to sleep – he knew if he fell asleep, he would lose the advantage of whatever head start he had over the Pinkertons. For surely, they too were going to wait for daybreak before tracking down the robbers, if they could.

There Jonah waited for the early grey of dawn.

He wiped the blood that had trickled down the back of his neck and ate both apples.

The early dawn came with a breeze, and the clouds were silvered. Jonah knew there would be a storm. It didn't take him long to pick up the trail – things he learned in the earlier days of the army - fresh torn earth over budding spring ground plants. The train scene was about half a mile behind him he could tell now and he knew he needed to get moving because the Pinkertons and marshal were sure to bring dogs, and some of them most likely on horseback.

He picked his way across the wood's floor, zigging from tree to tree, keeping the hoof prints of the robber's horses clear in his sight. And not long after, the ground elevated slightly.

How his head still ached. His eyesight wasn't one hundred percent and was thankful for the day's overcast. Had it been a sunny day, the direct light of the sun may have made things worse.

Jonah didn't get very far after the pitching land when he heard the flow of water. A stream nearby. He crept along quietly, and it seemed the tracks disappeared into the water. It hadn't even been an hour since he began tracking in the day, though he was moving at a quick pace. The sun was still very low in the east. The train and Pinkertons couldn't be more than a few miles away, Jonah guessed. He went to the water and took and long drink and splashed some of the cool water on his face. The drifter wet the back of his hair to wash out some of the matted blood, but he didn't waste much time on that.

Jonah stood up and sent his hand into his knapsack to grab at his ammo pouch – in it he felt a dozen or so rounds. As his eyes, freshly watered and washed, scanned the other bank and west down the waterline. Jonah froze in place when his eyes caught hold of something. He side-stepped behind a tree and peaked on.

There, just thirty feet away, was a man sitting against a tree, with a rifle in his hands.

Jonah's heart stopped for a moment but restarted once again when he was able to get a better look at the man through his blurred, but bettering vision. The man snored and sighed...

The man was asleep!

Jonah let out a slow and steady breath of relief.

In the back of his mind, Jonah wished this was merely a hunter out early to take a deer, but as the sun rayed through the branches, he could see blood spattered on the man's shirt. Blood that wasn't his or seemed to come from any injuries he had.

No, this man was a look-out. He knew a camp must be close.

He had the man dead bank. Jonah could hit a nickel from thirty feet away, but that wasn't his problem. The sound of his gun going off would most likely alert the other robbers, and Jonah wasn't sure how many of them there were. And not just the robbers, but the Pinkertons as well. They could hear the shot and come riding in and overrun them all – Jonah most likely being implemented with the robbery in some way given that he fled the scene.

The man mumbled in his sleep and shifted a bit. Jonah, still frozen in place, wouldn't let a hair twitch. But after a few heartbeats the man was still asleep and showed no other signs of waking.

Jonah, so very meticulously and slowly began moving toward the sleeping man. He could tell it wasn't Pete Vogal because Pete wore a light brown pinched-front hat, and this man had on a white hat – or rather, a hat that was once white, but had been mistreated in its tenure upon this criminal's head.

Every inch that Jonah went he prayed. Begging god in his mind to keep this robber entertained with dreams while he moved in.

Jonah made it to the man and put his hand on the handle of his knife that was horizontal at the small of his back.

He wondered what this man's role in the robber gang was. Did he kill any of those laid out bodies back at the train? Did he deserve to be knifed in his sleep? He could tell by his messed shirt that he was standing close to someone who had been shot – maybe he did deserve a knife in his sleep.

What was his name?

He asked himself that question several times before on the battlefield, where a man was killed for the color of his shirt and all other reasons be damned. But he pushed those thoughts from his head and brought his mind back to the task at hand.

After a brief moment, he let go of the blade's handle and drew out his gun, so quietly. He turned the gun over in his hand taking it by the barrel.

In one swift and sudden strike, Jonah sapped the sentry on the head. It was a loud knock, though the sound was no doubt abbreviated by the man's hat. Had it been direct contact with his skull, it would have been much louder.

The man groaned in his sleep but slumped over on his side.

"Yeah, wait 'til you wake up, you shit heel. I hope you're cross-eyed." He whispered to the unconscious man.

The crisp morning air went quiet again. The chirping birds didn't seem to notice and the slight sound of flowing water assumed its ownership of the area.

Jonah sat his pistol back into its holster.

He stood up and looked over the area, slowly looking for signs of the others. But he saw none. The man was facing east, toward the sun and train tracks beyond. Which meant, if this man was a sentry, the others were behind him on toward the west.

Jonah patted the man down before he moved on and found a few dollars on his person and a newly made gold ring with a red sparkler set on it. Jonah remembered Pete's accomplice ripping off the hand of the fancy woman across the aisle on the train. Jonah wasn't sure why, but he dropped the ring into his hidden vest pocket and stuff the cash into his boot. Maybe he felt like returning it if he could. Maybe if he couldn't get *his* money back, she would give him a reward?

But Jonah wasn't really worried about that – his eyes fell over the brand-new Henry repeater rifle still laying in the man's lap.

"Well, hello," Jonah whispered to himself, lifting the rifle into his hands. He checked its action and to assure it was loaded. He wiped off a bit of dirt that was on the barrel. He had five shots. Jonah smelled the end of the barrel and confirmed the scent of burned powder. The man had fired this gun, during the robbery most likely. He slung the rifle over his shoulder.

Jonah wasn't sure how close the camp was from the look-out, but he knew it couldn't be too far away. He drew his volcanic and holding above the water so his powder stayed dry, slipped into the stream. He did this to approach more silently, and to possibly throw off any scent if he were being tracked by dogs. In a crouched position, slowly letting the water bounced him along, he kept his eyes and ears sharp, the developing sun at his back. The water was cold. But not prison in winter cold, so he waded on.

That's when he smelled the campfire smoke.

Marshal August Bragstone arrived at the train just as the drifter was deciding what to do with the sleeping man.

It was just after eight o'clock in the morning, and there were bodies lying about – the gang remnants sprawled here and there, one even still laying in the office car, half of his brain thrown against the cabinets by a Pinkerton shotgun. The dead Pinkertons were arranged in a line, their bowler hats set upon their chests and their surviving brethren standing over them.

The captain of the Pinkertons, a man named McGillicuddy saw the marshal coming and walked from the group, moving away to meet him.

The marshal investigated the area from where he stood and saw a woman in a fine dress distraught and fanning herself. He approached her first and slid down from his saddle.

"Ma'am," he offered, tipping his hat.

The woman was beside herself, rambling under her breath. He could tell this was her first encounter with outlaws. He didn't pry into her affairs too much but did gather in a few short questions that she was bound for New Arbor and had been robbed of her jewelry. She noted that a man across from her seemed to know the bandits, but the bandits broke his head and made off with his folding money. And that when he came to, he went after them for justice.

The part that interested the marshal most however, that the stranger fled the scene and made off into the woods – in the same direction as the escaping raiders. Allegedly for "justice," but he had known some very clever criminals.

He asked if she had noticed him giving his name, but she did not.

He asked for his description, and she gave it.

He questioned the Western Union workers after that and learned that the man in question was a drifter and not part of their outfit, and despite being a "arrogant cunny," they didn't believe him to be party with the robbery. "Calling himself Jonah."

Just then the interview with the workers was cut short when the head Pinkerton approached.

"Good morning, marshal. I'm McGillicuddy, Pinkertons. You got here awfully fast," the captain said, as he made his way to him.

"Fast? How do you mean? Train got hit, I see." the marshal replied looking over all the carnage. Bullet holes in the train cars, glass shattered, and the train wheels and rails obviously blasted by dynamite. He walked the captain away from the witnesses to better contain their conversation they were about to have.

"We sent a couple horses back to get a hold of you, to come and handle the law side of this robbery. You aren't marshal Roberts, out of St Paul?"

"Son, I received no such word. I'm tracking an outlaw and have been for the last six weeks, I'm bound for New Arbor. August Bragstone, out of Kentucky." They shook hands.

The marshal looked around with a chuckle. The captain wasn't very pleased with this. In his rights, the captain could move on and track the robbers with his fellow Pinkertons, but they weren't hired as investigators

– their mission was protection and had slain officers. He needed local law enforcement to track down the criminals.

And the captain failed that mission.

And because he failed, that meant it was a matter of the law now. So, he would have to wait for the wired marshal. This did not please McGillicuddy, who would not break his contract with his client.

Marshal Bragstone went about the bodies of the fallen gang robbers. He didn't seem quite interested enough as he rolled the last of them over and knelt down over the corpse. He dropped his head and spit in the dirt.

The captain was clearly agitated, "We haven't entirely figured them for any known gangs, but we did notice this tattoo-"

"None are my man," he said to McGillicuddy standing, a twinge of disappointment and exhaustion in his voice. He went back to his horse.

"Marshal can you at least stay on until Mr. Roberts arrives? We aren't entirely sure what our play is here…"

"Roberts is a good man, he'll be along shortly, I'm sure – I'd worry more about getting that rattler moving and this track cleared."

"Best we can figure about three, maybe four, got away with the cashbox."

The marshal put his back to his horse as he turned on the captain.

"What cashbox?"

"Well, I'm not entirely at liberty to say," The captain began, but stopped mid-sentence when the lawman turned away from him again, rolling his eyes – clearly this Pinkerton wasn't hammered together all the way. The marshal's eyes then focused on the wild open forest along the tracks. He walked over the iron rails, seeing the horseshoes tracks that tore into the earth where the bandits made their escape – just where the woman had said.

He turned to the captain then, "What's next down the track? What town?"

"Nothing but small camps and forest and then the end of the line," he responded as he walked back to his people. "New Arbor. About half a day ride, but are you entirely sure this drifter they mentioned is heading for town? Looks like if he's your man he went off into the timber."

"Entirely."

The captain waved him off in frustration and stormed off. That gave Bragstone a smirk.

As the captain was walking away the marshal noticed coming around the bend far down the rails, maybe a half of a mile back, a small group of riders with dogs.

"That would be the marshal, captain," he murmured to himself, not caring.

New Arbor, at last. The marshal threw his leg up over his saddle, mounting his horse. He turned his horse toward the forest and again found the tracks leading off and away from the train scene. A distant roll of thunder promised rain. Follow the rails or follow the bandits? If this drifter was his man Dade that he was after, and not this "Jonah", which he suspected was a fake name, he knew that eventually he would need to resurface in the town. All that money and no supplies? And New Arbor was the end of the line.

He decided to follow into the forest. Their head start wasn't so grand, and Bragstone was one man tracking. They no doubt stopped somewhere to rest in the night, which if he was lucky, their camp was closer than these Pinkerton's could guess.

But he needed to ride fast. New Arbor was only a day's ride away by rails and if the rain coming in was a down pour, he could lose the bandit's tracks. After the town there was nothing but the Dakota Nation for a thousand miles and then Manitoba and the Northwest Territories beyond. If the drifter made it passed New Arbor before the marshal could get to him, he would have let his man slip away.

Time was against him. He gave his horse an added spurring.

He was running out of civilized country.

Jonah crept his way along the river, using the sound of it to cover his movement. It wasn't long before the thick scent of the smoke was accompanied by the soft jangle of saddled horses. Jonah moved to the bank, the sun still at his back. He delicately slipped from the water, taking great care to not splash or let himself be heard. He crawled on his belly up the bank of the stream and once at the top, removed his hat. He tilted his head to the side and lifted his neck to scan the area.

Three of them and four horses. The fire had died down to mostly large, glowing embers.

All three men were asleep. Pete and Gavin were facing Jonah, and the third of them had his back to him – he was only a few paces away.

The horses were still saddled, no doubt they left them that way should they need to rise quickly and make a run for it. But best they figured the law would take time to arrive at the train, which was only a few miles back.

On the large brown horse, was a box shaped object, maybe the size of a milk box. It was wrapped and tied tight through the saddle straps. Whatever it was they kept it secure and close. And then Jonah remembered the Irish worker and what he said. They were heading for New Arbor to install line poles for Western Union. And then he mentioned a rumor about a company being purchased. It seems that Pete and his gang had heard that rumor as well and drew their plans. Jonah's eyes lit up as he made the connections in his mind – it was the Western Union payroll at the very least – and possibly even the cashbox to purchase the lumber camp.

Pete could keep the measly seven hundred dollars, Jonah thought, grinning.

But how to steal it? A shootout with three men? Yes, they were sleeping, and he could take care of them all, but again the sound of his gun going off would bring in the Pinkertons and the law. No, he thought shaking the thought away.

So Jonah just silently shrugged and slipped through the camp without making a single sound. He put his boot into the stirrup and gently pulled himself up into the saddle. He hadn't made a single sound, and he whisperlessly took the reins in his hands and nudged the horse away. Its hooves clopped and it snorted, but still the three men didn't wake.

And as misfortune would have it, a loud clap of thunder rented the morning air.

The third man shot up out of his dead sleep, a look of terror on his face, as if he had woke from a horrible dream. His eyes drifted around then and met with Jonah's, a look of pure confusion

Then realization.

Then rage!

The third man hopped up to his feet and went for his gun.

"They'll hear you, fool!" Jonah warned with a harsh whisper.

His voice stirred the other two.

The third man didn't care at all in that moment. His rage clearly clouding his judgement, he went for the draw. Jonah, still holding onto his volcanic, had no choice but to let it erupt.

The gun blast put everyone into a panic.

The third man's head rocked back and forth violently as Jonah's shot went through his forehead. He collapsed forward, face down on to the burning embers.

Pete went for his gun, Gavin grabbed at his knife, but Jonah was already kicking the horse and hauling away the swag. Pete took two shots – the first missed, the second would have been true enough to strike Jonah in the lower back, but the bullet sparked off the metal box.

Jonah already had the horse at full speed when he heard the first of Pete's bullets whiz by, had the bullet been any closer to his head it would have taken his ear off.

"Gavin, get the horses!"

"What about Stevie!?"

"Fuck 'em, he's dead," Pete said as he mounted his horses and kicked it on. Gavin followed suit as they went after Jonah.

They could see him way down the stream on Stevie's horse, blasting through the water. Jonah had a good head start. Pete locked his teeth and kicked his horse bloody. He wanted to kill Jonah so bad he could taste it.

Stevie's shirt licked fire, the sound of his blood hissed as it poured onto the embers.

A man crept through the thickets along the stream, making his way to the campsite.

The campsite where he was to meet the Vogals, whom he hired to rob the train.

The man was in his sixties, early sixties. He had long clean hair and a red eyepatch over his left eye.

As he got close, he heard a gun go off and men started shouting. Then more gun fire. The man drew his own pistol as he rushed through the brush. As he came out the other side, could see the campsite. Two Vogals he recognized chasing after another who seemed to have the cashbox – they rushed down the shallow stream. The man with the cashbox he couldn't rightly see so well, but he could tell he had a good head start.

The man, Getty by name, quickly inspected the campsite and saw that the third man was dead and smoldering. And the rest of the gang were missing. He didn't know who this man was taking off with the money. Was there a mutiny? Or were they followed? A Pinkerton? Too many questions and not enough answers.

He slipped back into the brush, disappearing. Getty made his way back to the place he left his horse. Just then it started to rain.

Mother would need to hear about this.

And she would not be pleased.

Marshal Bragstone walked his horse along, following the tracking in the dirt. He had been at it over an hour when suddenly in the far distance he heard the gun fire. The marshal threw his leg over his mount, and kicked his horse on in the direction of the distant fracas.

Ten minutes later he slowed his pace knowing he must be close.

When he saw a man in a dirty old white hat slumped over at the base of a tree he stopped his mount altogether and dismounted.

He approached the man briskly, thinking him dead – he had blood on his shirt.

But when the marshal got up close, he heard the man groan in his sleep, bringing a shaking hand up to his head. The man rolled more over and was now flat on his back.

"What in god's name happened?" The downed man fought for each word.

"Where is the cashbox?" the marshal asked. Best to start with questions while this one was confused – maybe he would give something up.

"What? Who the hell…" The man was barely able to speak. He didn't recognize the voice as one of his cohorts.

"Where is the cashbox?"

The marshal stood over the helpless man, his eyes raking the surroundings for clues.

The man creaked open one eye barely, looking up at the badge.

"You go to Hell, lawdog."

"I reckon they're off to the west, since you're facing east, eh boy?" the marshal said, not hearing the downed robber even in the slightest. Nor did he want or expect a response to his rhetorical question.

The man groaned again, pulling the marshal from his thoughts.

The marshal then lifted his foot and put the space between his boot heel and toes exactly over the man's Adam's apple.

And then put all of his weight on it, forcing downward.

The man's eyes popped open, and he began struggling, grabbing at the marshal's boot and leg, desperately trying to get him off his throat. He looked up strangling to death, through bulging eyes. His legs kicked in useless abandon. The man expected to perhaps be arrested or interrogated, but not this. The look on his face was both surprise and terror.

He looked up to see the cold blue eyes of the marshal watching him slowly die.

And after a brief fight for his life, which he lost, the man stopped struggling and went limp.

The marshal pulled his boot away and hooked his thumbs into his gun belt.

"Yeah, I reckon off into the west is where that fracas occurred."

And he stepped away and mounted his horse.

The marshal continued on until he smelled a mix of burning flesh and campfire smoke. The stench was thick in the air, despite the pre-storm breeze. He pulled a bandana from his coat and covered his nose and mouth with it.

He found the camp and saw that it was deserted. The bed rolls were still out, the stew pot uncleaned, and a man burning face down in the fire. Whatever happened here, he suspected some form of disagreement and they let out fast.

Maybe this one in the fire was a planned killing so they could increase their cut?

He saw their tracks lead off toward the stream and he realized that he lost them.

The man face-down in the fire couldn't be Dade – wrong height. This man in the fire couldn't have been more than five and half feet, and portly. Dade was tall and thin.

And just then it started to rain.

"Damn," he said to himself.

Chasing at this point was moot, the marshal realized. He lost them. He lost their tracks hurrying off to the stream and he would lose their tracks in the rain even if he did pick up the trail again.

He spit to the ground and turned his horse about, disappointed with his luck.

The marshal would have to backtrack to the train and follow the rails to New Arbor.

Just then he heard the baying of hound dogs in the distance.

"Marshal Roberts, I presume," he muttered to himself.

Bragstone wanted nothing to do with these men. He had his answers, and his destination was set. Any further delays would only be more of an advantage to Dade – or this Jonah, as he called himself.

He kicked his horse off to the north and was long out of sight before the pack of tracking bloodhounds descended on the campsite.

*M*arshal Ashley Roberts, leading the dogs, shouted his men on ahead.

The men found a smoldering body, a dead lookout man whose throat was crushed in and a single horse tied to a tree. The campsite suddenly abandoned. A young deputy vomited when they turned over Stevie's burnt body, the rain did little to dull the smell.

"My God," the marshal said, taking the cigar from his mouth and shaking his head in appalment.

After nearly an hour of picking through the campsite and wrapping up the bodies, marshal Roberts took a long chew on his sopping cigar and called it. There was no cashbox to be found, and the dogs had lost the scent at the water's edge. All they found at the camp was vigorous death. Ashley Roberts was seventy years old and he had been a lawman for nearly fifty of them, but he rarely came across a scene like this – nothing this brutal. Maybe in his earlier days when he dealt with the Indians, but nothing recent after taking his appointment in St. Cloud. There was nothing else he could do there at the campsite and the storm had them all drenched.

"Ok, boys, lets head back to the train and regroup," he said. "This is a dead end. Put them bodies on that spare horse and we'll get 'em buried."

The marshal took in a deep breath and sighed it out, scAnning the camp one last time. It wasn't often that a robbery was successfully executed, but when it was he took it personally.

This investigation would take a while, marshal Roberts realized.

He would drink whiskey that night.

*J*onah rode down the stream for at least a mile and then cut up into the small hills. He looked back through the storm from time to time and he could see that Pete and Gavin were following him. Eventually, they would catch him. They were gaining, slowly but surely.

Jonah couldn't really see Pete's face, but by how he was riding with pure determination he could tell that Pete wasn't in the mood for a discussion.

An hour later Jonah broke the tree line and came onto a wide open field of tall grass. The rain had stopped by then and the sun brought with it a fresh humidity.

All of their horses gleaming with perspiration, Pete pulled the rifle from his saddle. Gavin had no rifle, but he drew his revolver anyway. Pete took his first shot, and though Jonah was over a hundred yards away, the bullet ripped into the horses hind quarters, its tendons snapping. It whinnied in terrible pain and its entire rear gave out, throwing Jonah over the side. Jonah came down hard on his shoulder and ribs, tumbling off into the next thick brush on the tree line. Never losing consciousness, Jonah was quick to crawl for cover behind a large rock and keep the rifle in his off-hand. He could hear the two fast approaching, hooting and hollering. Jonah, pulling back his holster's weather flap, drew his gun and sent two quick shots toward Pete and Gavin.

The robbers pulled back hard on their reigns and after a fast dismount dove behind an old collapsed shack. Jonah had taken away their momentum.

They were only one hundred feet apart or so, but the sun by now had hit noon and Jonah, under the tree line had the advantage of shadow cover. Pete and Gavin were out in the open, laughing loud enough for their prey to hear.

"You ain't got no way outta this, Jonah, you son of a bitch!" Pete said. Gavin took a shot that whizzed off of Jonah's rock.

Jonah steadied himself with a deep breath. He flexed the hand of his numb shoulder. He was sure no bones had broken buy he did hit the ground hard. He peeked around the side of the rock to take in the situation.

The two robbers came from cover and sent a volley of several shots, Jonah dropped his head and felt two of the bullet's vibration strike the rock. Immediately, Jonah came up, this time with the rifle he had taken from the look-out man, and squeezed off a single shot.

The dull thud of a bullet breaking into flesh and bone came echoing back across the field.

Gavin dropped with a groan, having been hit in his shooting shoulder. The blood from the wound spattered across Pete's face, hunkered next to him. Gavin's gun falling to the ground from his grasp and landing at Pete's feet.

Pete cursed his name again and sent the rest of his rifle rounds in Jonah's direction, but the drifter had already retaken his cover.

"Hey Pete!" Jonah called out. "Let's be reasonable! Your man is bleeding out and will be dead in a matter of minutes!"

Pete turned quickly to Gavin and could see a look a horror cross his face. Gavin gripped his gushing shoulder hard and let out a whimper, "Don't let me die here, Pete," he begged, his voice breaking.

"Don't you believe that bastard, Gav," Pete insisted as he reloaded, "I seen folks shot way worse than you and make it."

"Yeah, but he ain't goin' to make it way out here without a doctor!" Jonah spoke out. The drifter checked his rifle…only four shots left…

The blood was draining from Gavin's face and he groaned out for God.

"You shut up, you card cheatin' whore!" Pete screamed. He put his last bullet in the receiver and sent five shots into the brush wear Jonah hunkered down. A rage of lead and revenge.

After, it felt quiet.

Jonah didn't come back with a response. After several heart beats of adrenaline, Pete looked over to Gavin and shrugged.

When the smoke cleared, there lay Jonah's hat and his pistol fallen over the top of the rock. Pete's eyes went wide.

"Ha! I got him, Gav!" he cackled with wicked laughter. "You're goin' be just fine cousin." He assured him. "And rich!"

Gavin struggled through the pain, somehow able to smirk slightly. The sun blinded him.

Pete hopped up, drawing his pistol and ran over to the rock to put one more bullet in that son of a bitch that dared cross his path.

He was Pete Vogal – killer of men.

Gavin's face was already feverish. He had never been shot before and the torn and burning flesh locked up his body with fear. The amount of blood lustering under the high and unclouded sun sent his mind into shock. He was sure he was going to die, but maybe Pete could get him to a doctor in time. Maybe this field was an old farm with folks still living there that could help him. His breathing came in labors, the pain was relentless. He could feel the bullet burning inside his shoulder. He had never been so thirsty in all of his life.

Gavin heard a single shot. And he sighed heavily in relief.

"Did you get him!" Gavin cried out. He was flat on his back, the sun in his eyes.

"Pete, God damnit, did you get him?"

He heard spurred steps coming his way through the grass, and a tall shadow fell over him.

"Yeah," a hatless Jonah said calmly, levering his last bullet into the chamber, "I got him."

Gavin Vogal never heard the shot that killed him.

*M*arshall Bragstone rode hard all that day, back-tracking.

As the sun began to set it was blotted over by another ravenous storm. As he passed the last water pump for the rail traffic he knew he was but only a handful of hours away from town. He knew he would be arriving after dark.

He had no delusions of beating the weather to town, as he and the coming storm surged toward each other. When he was but only two miles away, and passed the first out-laying farmstead, the rain began to bucket down.

Jonah rode on the rest of that day, mostly moving north toward this town of New Arbor – or at least where he guessed it was. Hopefully he would cross the train rails again and take them in. His head, shoulders and ribs ached. It had been a full day for the drifter, but he had a cashbox with him and a healthy horse – having taken one of the Vogal mounts, though it took him nearly an hour to run the animal down.

He came upon a pond that was fed by a stream. He didn't think it was the same stream that was along the campsite of the bandits, but he couldn't be sure. The sun was near setting and it seemed yet another round of weather was going to blow through.

He needed shelter, and he needed to open and bury this cashbox.

It was time to stop. And this pond seemed just as good a place as any.

Getty knew these lands better than any marshal from Kentucky or any drifter wounded and ambling through the countryside.

He made it home an hour before dark - an old estate outside of New Arbor on Cottau Lake, where his entire family lived.

He wasn't sure how many Gettys there were now, with all the grandchildren and great grandchildren, and he didn't really care. The Gettys had been there for four generations – began as a distillery outpost for hunters and Indians – and soldiers who tried pushing the frontier west, but the Minnesota Territory had held its shape for many years.

When he pulled his horse into the stable an early teenaged girl was there to take it from him. Her name was Lily Ann, but he got that wrong half the time. And that was only when he needed to speak to her. This man, Uncle Roge, as he was known, didn't waste his breath with cordials.

He was only known as Uncle Roge, because Roger Getty sired no children of his own – none who now lived, anyway.

She watched him stomp off and then pushed his horse into its stall. She didn't like her uncle Roge, none of the younger Gettys did. They would tell ghost stories about him. About how he fought for the south in the war and killed many blacks – both soldier and slave. And how he used to have two sons, but one was killed in the war and the other died before he was two years old.

Stories about how he lost his eye to a black witch's voodoo curses many years ago, and how that none of the younger children had seen him without his patch – but some of the older Getty grand children made such claims.

A distant rumble of more thunder echoed distantly across the lake.

She closed up the stall and scampered off to see if dinner was nearly done.

Roger Getty made his way in to the estate, coming in the eastern entrance that lead through the kitchen.

There were several women cooking and preparing the evening feast that would feed the entire Getty clan. Some were wives of Getty sons, other were sisters.

Roger had no wife – not one who lived anyway.

The smell was pleasing to him, but only for a fleeting moment. His focus was mainly on what he would say to mother and how he would explain that the plan didn't go as designed.

He came into the main entrance of the house and turned a corner where his brother John was at the base of the grand stair waiting.

Roger stopped when John put himself into his path.

"Well?"

Roger glared at him with his one good eye. A glare firm enough to back John down a bit. John was the oldest Getty male and heir to the estate, but Roger was by far more dangerous a man. They both knew this –

they both also knew that mother would not tolerate in-fighting amongst the siblings. John used this, and this alone to flex his seniority. But if it came down to a scrape, John knew Roger would whip him good.

"You don't seem to be carrying with you a large sum money, little brother" John offered.

"Stand aside, I need to see mother."

"And she will see you when she is ready. She was already in bed, but when she heard you were approaching she called on Jane to help fix her back up."

"Move," was all Roger offered.

John held up his hands and let him pass.

Roger went up the center of the stairs, careful to not touch the polished banister.

Mother didn't like smudges on her polished woodwork – which could be found all throughout the estate.

He made it to the top and went down a long corridor of a hallway. At the end were a set of, again polished, double doors.

He removed his hat and took a breath, convincing himself it wasn't his fault.

Roger gently knocked on the door. He could hear muffled voices inside.

Then the door opened and there stood his sister Jane, the second oldest Getty. She had already lit her candle, as the sun was setting and a storm approached. And several candelabras burned in the room, as well as a fire in the fireplace.

Of all the siblings he had, nine in total, Roger got along best with Jane. They had a childhood bond that went into them being adults. While Roger was off fighting in the war, it was Jane he wrote to, not mother. While John was the oldest, and constantly being groomed by mother and their late father, Jane and Roger were left to raise the other Getty children. And between Roger and Michael, the fourth Getty child, there were near five years difference.

He walked past her and they shared a look. Jane could tell nothing good had happened, so she decided to stay. She closed the doors behind them.

Roger despised coming to this room. The ingrained smells of old perfume and dust and dog. The dozen or so mannequins about the place, their arms distorted or missing, draped over with dresses abandoned halfway through their making. Aged from a Paris-white to a brown of burned grass.

There, sitting up in her bed, was the venerable Mother Getty. She wore a fashionable black wig and had a powdered face, though the covering did nothing to cloak her age, which was eighty-six.

Next to her in bed, always on guard, was Judge, her old and ever faithful shepherd hound.

"So, Uncle Roge has returned," she said, scratching Judge behind his ear. Her voice was rasped and flat. She wore a smirk exposing her black teeth and her sunken dark eyes peered out. "Take it off, you know I don't like it."

Roger cleared his throat and removed his eye patch. He never liked taking it off, especially in front of anyone, but if he could say he was comfortable in front of anyone without it, it would be Jane.

"There's my boy's beautiful face." She said, her voice always cold though she tried to project warmth – a false warmth.

His eye was completely ripped away, leaving only a dull and empty lavender socket. Stabbed out by a runaway slave.

"Now...how did it go?"

Roger looked her in the eyes because he knew better than to not.

"There was a complication, mother," he said firmly, with confidence. "It seems the train was hit, as it hasn't arrived yet. But when I went to the meeting place a man took off with the box. Two Vogals chased him, I believe."

"What man?" she asked. Her tone began to edge toward anger. "You *believe?"*

"I'm not certain. It happened just as I arrived. I wasn't seen."

"And you chose not to pursue because you are stupid." She said through gritted teeth. Judge issued a low growl.

"No, mother, I chose not to pursue because if I had been spotted by the law, who were sure to follow, our family would have been implemented in the robbery."

Mother relaxed back against the polished headboard of her regal bed. She calmed Judge's edge with more comfort behind his ear.

A moment passed before mother spoke again, both siblings holding perfectly quiet. They knew better than to speak if mother was thinking, and mothers anger sometimes came with fresh scars from Judge. Several grand children hated that old dog for that very reason. They felt no love from it or grandmother Getty.

"Is this man who took our money heading this way?" she said, calm and only mildly cold again – her fake warmth.

"I believe so. New Arbor is the only town for miles and because of the gunfire, he may be wounded."

Mother nodded in agreement.

"Have our kin watch out for the Vogals or this other man. Whoever shows up first won the race."

She knew that money was out there somewhere and the Gettys needed it. The rumors were true about Deward selling the lumber mill to Western Union, mother Getty understood, so they wouldn't renegotiate the same deal she had with Deward for a stake in the lumber company – her lease would be broken, and as far as compensation, whatever Deward owed her at that point wouldn't last long. Selling the land outright to Western Union wasn't an option. And the whiskey distillery couldn't sustain or feed a clan of nearly fifty people.

They needed that money. To progress the family into politics or at least to buy a handful of politicians. They needed a new way to survive and thrive, and this was the plan.

With that, she waved him off. The conversation was over.

Just then the rain had arrived and was beginning to patter on the glass of her windows.

Roger turned on his heel and headed for the door. He shared another look to Jane and they both thought the same thing. The same thing they always thought when dealing with mother in such ways.

She can't live forever.

Roger closed the door behind him, leaving his sister to tend to mothers turning down for the evening.

In the hall, he replaced his eye patch and then his hat.

John wasn't hard to find.

Penny Landon walked the breadth of her office and placed another receptacle on the floor to catch the rain sneaking through the ceiling. The storm came late in the day, near sundown and though it rained for only an hour so far, it was the fourth receptacle she had put down. A quick glance out the dark window was momentarily lit with a flash of lightning and she could see the street outside was already covered in puddles – the river would swell, she knew. She just prayed any new-comers had the sense to wait it out rather than getting their wagon stuck and her needing to send Mandle and Old Zach to pull them out.

She had been elected sheriff six years prior when her father, her predecessor, had passed away at the venerable age of seventy nine. He, James Landon, had been sheriff of Douglas County for as long as New Arbor had been there. Though in those days it was called Whiskey Hills, and it was more or less an outpost for the Getty family, and the distillery they owned there. But in 1856, Eunice and Ruth Deward purchased the river and timber land, their east coast connections quickly brought in new businesses, and the town was renamed New Arbor. They asked James Landon to be the mayor but he was a law man, not a government man – and if you asked James, there was a difference.

Sheriff Penny made it back to her desk and dropped into her creaking chair. She took up the newspaper on her desk, but before picking back up with the story on a dead child found in Minneapolis, she looked over to the drunk in the first cell.

Dougy Getty, his chin beard matted with blood, lay flat on his back and snored away like a blacksmith bellow.

Penny sighed heavily and put her feet up on the desk, opening the paper.

Catherine Howard at Pence Opera House, April 18.

The sheriff had never seen an opera or even heard one. She wondered what compelled fancy folks to attend such outings. Penny never cared for art or music. Her father was a law man and so was his father before him. She had a brother with whom her father had high expectations, but when Mandle turned five and still could barely speak, it was clear to him that he wouldn't follow in the family work. But as it were, James Landon raised his daughter as if she were a boy – it was all he knew since mother passed while giving birth to Mandle.

Penny didn't recall her mother very much, she was only four years old.

She went on reading a bit longer and the storm worsened. Dougy Getty stirred having nearly choked himself awake from his snoring. That gave Penny a mildly frustrating pause. She lowered her paper and looked across the way to the dark cell.

It was barely spring and the Gettys were already at it, starting their trouble a bit early this year. There were nine Gettys, under their mother Mary who still lived out at Cottau Lake. Penny wasn't sure exactly how old Mary was, but she knew old man Getty, that's Edgar Getty, died near twenty years ago. The way Penny figured it, Mary could very well be ninety years old – an astonishing feat.

She sighed heavily and gave her newspaper an annoyed flap to straighten it.

This was already the second bar brawl of the spring and the seasonal workers for the Deward Lumber Company had yet to arrive. But that train was due any time now – in fact, thinking on it, Penny realized the train was late.

And to add to that, the Western Union people were coming this year as well, to put up their telegraph lines and the railroad was already sending surveyors out west into the Dakota territory to expand through Wyoming – but on top of it all there was a rumor that

Deward made a deal with Western Union, but that was just whore hear-say.

Yes, it was going to be a long summer Penny realized.

Just then the door swung open and the raging storm outside flashed and roared. Penny looked out over the top of her news paper, and in the door she expected her brother Mandle – who was also her deputy, amongst several other odd town jobs – but instead was a tall shadowy figure.

He turned and closed the door. He removed his drenched duster and hat.

"Is this weather normal for this time of year this far north?" the man said with an edge of levity.

"Can I help you?" was all Penny offered.

"Ah, yes indeed. I'm Marshal August Bragstone, out of Lexington, Kentucky. Can you lead me to the sheriff, please ma'am."

Penny didn't say anything, she just lowered her paper and let the lamp light glisten off the star on her breast. She wasn't accustomed to strangers arriving in this drenching Hell weather, nor in the middle of the night, to boot. Her paper was set down on the desk in front of her and her hands appeared to come to rest on the arms of the chair, but really Penny put them into the shadow so they could be closer to the gun that dangled at her hip.

The marshal gave a slight surprised look, arriving to this edge of civilization kind of town to find a woman enforcing the law. He made a mental note that this lady was not to be spoken down to or underestimated – if she is the sheriff of these parts, she can perhaps hold her own.

Penny had been used to this look her entire life. But at length the marshal shrugged and simply said, "Very well."

"Mind the buckets," she said, and the marshal dodged two of them as he made his way to the opposite side of her desk.

He held out his hand, "August Bragstone."

"Penny Landon." She said, taking it for a moment.

The marshal noticed a calloused characteristic to her handshake – he would be right to respect this woman.

Penny motioned for him to take a seat.

"So, what brings you this far north, marshal?"

"Got a man I'm tracking, out of Chicago most recently. Name of William Dade."

"Uh huh, and what's on his menu?"

"Robbery, kidnapping, impersonating an officer and murder," he said matter-of-factly. "I've been on him for several days now, but I got information that he had left Chicago and was heading north and west on a train."

"What made him abandon the securities of the city?"

"Oh, every time they take to the drink it's a dick measuring contest with no room for second place."

The marshal looked up suddenly, realizing that may have been offensive to say in the company of a lady.

Penny gave a slight chuckle, seeing him realize his breach of etiquette.

"Yes, marshal, men have dicks. You'll have to try harder than that to offend me."

They both shared a smirk at that. The marshal liked this Sheriff Penny. The thought of a woman sheriff may normally turn up his nose, and most others' noses as well, but she seemed to have a good head on her shoulders for the job and she certainly isn't shaken by a stranger arriving in the dark of a storm.

"Very well then, sheriff, thank you," he conceded. "Where was I?"

"William Dade heading this way."

"Yes, indeed," he said. "So, in case you haven't realized it yet due to the storm, your last train is late."

Penny nodded and pulled out her father's pocket watch. "I did notice that the last runner was behind – see we're expecting seasonal workers to arrive for the lumber mill."

"Well, Im sorry to be the bearer of bad news, sheriff but that train was robbed. And several people were killed."

Penny shook her head slowly and let out a sigh. She then motioned for him to continue.

"Well, I believe my man was on that train when it was robbed."

"Involved?"

"Possibly, but I don't believe so, but then again this character is a clever one. Testimony from two witnesses say a 'drifter' was recognized by the robbers and they busted his head pretty good, then took a large wad of bills from his inner pocket. After, the drifter went out a window and took off into the night to follow his robbers. And if theyre heading this way, trouble with this drifter is sure to follow."

"Why come here?"

"You know the type, Im sure, sheriff. Cant stay away from the sins of civilization. Always tempted. Hell, if it weren't for men like that the world wouldn't need law dogs like us."

Penny rocked back in her chair and let out another heavy sigh.

"Great…" was all she offered at the moment. This was exactly what she needed to help the Gettys kick off their summer. But in that moment she refused. She made a silent oath to herself just then that this town would be a quiet one for just one summer. Just one season of peace and quiet, when the lumber workers could have a good time at a poker table and no Gettys flipping tables and hollering about their daddy building this town. Truth of it was the Landons had been there just as long.

Penny had no idea how wrong she would be.

Just then the office door opened and in came the wind.

"Jesus and Joseph," the marshal said quietly to himself, slowly standing to his feet.

In came the deputy, dragging another man by his boot. The man was either passed out drunk or beaten into submission - the marshal couldn't tell which. Had it not been for the poor man's groaning, the marshal may have assumed the man dead.

The deputy was perhaps the biggest man he had ever seen. Giant blue eyes and sopping wet from the storm. His shirt was covered in blood and it looked like he took a couple licks himself. He had to be near seven feet tall, but it was the deputy's mass that staggered the marshal. He found himself letting out a small chuckle at the sheer amazement in this man's volume.

"Marshal August – my brother, deputy Mandle Landon," Penny said. She could see the effect that her brother had on the marshal, and it was exactly what she wanted. It's exactly why she kept him close.

"Howdy," the marshal said, extending his hand for a shake.

"Hello, sir," Mandle offered back. When he took the marshal's hand it seemed to disappear. The marshal let out a single "*Ha!*"

The deputy then went back to dragging the man farther inside. He didn't take him to a cell however, but to the cot that Penny kept in the office just in case a guard was required at all hours.

"Who do we have here?" Penny said going over with her lantern. "Ah," she said, kneeling down and placing the lantern on the floor. "Andy Johnson, what in the hell did you do? Get in a fight with a bear?"

Andy Johnson just groaned and barely got out, "God damn Gettys."

Penny sighed and stood up. She looked at the marshal and shrugged.

"The Getty Gang," she explained to the marshal. "A local family of shit-heels that have been here since the town's founding. Troublemakers. They have the distillery here in town just across the street there, and they own land that's leased to the lumber mill."

The marshal nodded his head, understanding completely. There was a bushel of bad apples in every town in America it seemed to him – and he had been to many towns. But if not for men like them…

"Well marshal August," Penny said reluctantly, "I was going to offer you the cot here, but I think Mr. Johnson would appreciate it a bit more."

"No ma'am, I'm fine with a hotel if you just point me the way," the marshal said politely.

"Two buildings down is the Dragoon Saloon, they have rooms – but that's where these two came from," Penny said. "Or you can ride out here and go the other way. When you see the church make a right and that's a more quiet, but expensive, establishment. Just rooms there, no watering."

It didn't take the marshal long to make that decision.

"I reckon I'll buy for the quiet," he said. And they all nodded it to be a good choice.

Mandle had just gently laid Andy Johnson on the cot and went into the back without another word. He looked tired to Penny and maybe got some dents of his own. She let him go out the back.

"Well good night to you, sheriff," the marshal said. "quite an operation you got here," he couldn't help another chuckle. "Family law?"

"Yes sir, my father was sheriff of this county since fifty-eight when Minnesota entered the union."

"I'm sure he's proud of you," the marshal offered turning toward the door.

Penny smiled just a scratch.

As he put on his duster and hat the sheriff said after to him, "Regarding this drifting murderer business, marshal. I want to keep it quiet. No need to rowdy up my town with worry."

Marshall Bragstone turned slowly back toward her and tipped his hat. "I'll come by in the morning and we'll go over the details."

With that, he went back out into the storm. He threw his leg over his horse and started plopping along the muddied street toward the hotel.

The marshal thought again about the deputy and mans sheer size. How he effortlessly pulled the beaten brawl victim and set him on the cot. The man's strength was inhuman – more like a draft horse powering a large tree stump from the earth.

He made a very strict mental note to never underestimate or anger deputy Mandle. Or sheriff Penny, who held his reigns.

The canvas wrapping the cashbox was in fact a small tent, Jonah realized. And he had it set up before the rain hit. Though it had a couple holes in it, it was keeping him dry enough.

Jonah needed a light source so he got a small fire going with a bit of his pistol necessities. The wind outside began to pick up a bit, and he wondered if the tent would hold, given he had to use make-shift branches for tent poles.

In the dim of the light though, these thoughts were fleeting. Huddled in the back of the meager shelter was the metal cashbox.

He took a deep breath and spun it slowly around so the lock could face him.

"*Ha!*" he said aloud to himself. It appeared that when Jonah first let out of the Vogals camp and Pete took two wild shots at him, that one of the bullets, the one that the box intercepted, had struck the iron lock and left it derelict.

"Well hell, thanks, Pete."

He slid his knife away to the small of his back and after giving the lock a mediocre shake, pulled it off. In his hands it fell into two pieces.

He looked over his shoulder, out the single tent flap and into the storm. There he saw only the pond when it was lit up by lightning strike.

The drifter waited for the dark, and tossed the lock into the middle of the pond. He barely heard it splash over the torrential downpour.

He breathed a bit of heat into his hands, rubbed them together and flipped open the heavy metal lid.

"Mary be merciful…"

The drifter gazed down through unblinking eyes at a few tightly packed units of five-hundred dollar bills. He had never seen five hundred dollars bills, they were new and very crisp. He noticed that these weren't Bank of New York notes, but federally printed paper money. He licked his index and thumb and slid one out.

There, on the back, was a familiar face. Maj. Gen. Joseph Mansfield, honored in all his glory.

Jonah was there when the general was mortally wounded at the Battle of Sharpsburg. Having rushed forward believing his men were firing upon other Union soldiers, he found out otherwise when a lead ball ripped into his chest.

"Damned fool," the drifter said. He tucked the bill back into the stack with the others. He could hear the echoes of the canon and rifle fire then, the screaming, the men in grey, begging for their lives as Union bayonets spilled their insides. The man next to Jonah, a boy of sixteen named McDurin, who had been in America for only a few weeks...

He forced the thoughts away of the young soldier's early demise.

Jonah took a deep breath and refocused on the task at hand.

This wasn't merely a payroll delivery for the lumbermill, or Western Union workers.

He turned and peaked out of the tent flap into the storm. Scanning the pond perimeter to verify he was indeed alone. Through the clips of lightning he saw only nature.

After several heartbeats, Jonah blinked and returned to the box. He began further inspecting of it and found that tucked into a flap of the lid was a document folder, wrapped in leather.

With still hands, he calmly unraveled the leather strap securing it and opened the accordion-like folder.

Inside were documents, signed and officiated with lawyers representing the Western Union Company in New York City and a space left blank to be signed by a man named Ulysses W. Deward, president of the Deward Lumber Company. It was a contract of sales transferring all rights of land and business to Western Union for the agreed upon sum of…

"One hundred thousand dollars," Jonah breathed.

The drifter, a man who trekked deep into the Rocky Mountains making trails that no white man had ever seen, lived through the hell of prison for fifteen months, crossed the land fighting in the raining fire of war and took on a life of wandering since, sat back slowly and closed the lid.

He didn't move for many moments, his thoughts moving in a way that matched the storm just outside the tent flap as his life moved across his mind. This wasn't a paltry six or seven hundred dollars, transported for the payroll of the mill workers. This was wealth. This was a life of wanting for nothing ever again – if a drifter like Jonah could stretch twenty dollars over a month, this amount would potentially change everything he knew about life, let alone life itself. Could this change life in a way that made life worth living…and not just surviving? Or tolerating?

It would also have him running for the rest of that life. Hiding his identity, conjuring up lies as to how he came into such a fortune. He would be looking over his shoulder forever.

And how long before gangs, bounty hunters or even gun-fighters heard about the missing "Deward Fortune" and come looking to collect?

How many more Pete Vogals would he have to kill?

The Western Union people wouldn't let this go easily, he realized. Nor would this man Deward who has no doubt by now realized the train didn't arrive on time and the Pinkertons let the delivery slip through their fingers.

And the Pinkertons! Jonah had a run in with them not long ago and it wasn't a pleasant one. People knew better than to tangle with those thugs in badges.

Return it and hope for a reward, or take his chances and make a run for it like he always has.

Was he finally getting tired of running?

Because in truth, when Jonahs eyes first laid upon all that money he didn't feel joy or relief or justice for a life of hardship.

He felt fear. And exhaustion.

Men who had little money respected it. And men who didn't, lost it all.

He started digging a hole to bury it.

The following morning Jonah was awakened by a gun shot. He sprang off the ground, pistol in hand and came to the edge of the ten flap, the hammer on his volcanic ready to go. The storm had blown over and the sun glistened off the tops of the trees. It was still quite early.

He peeked outside.

He heard a deep bellow laughter, and on the other side of the pond a large black man bending down and scooping up a rabbit from the mouth of an old blue tick hound. Then he stuffed the dead coney in a burlap bag that was slung over his shoulder.

Jonah let out a sigh of relief and slid his pistol away. Just a local hunter and his dog. He grabbed up the few things that were laying about under the tent and began packing up his horse.

At this he heard a whistle from across the way. When he turned the black man held up a friendly hand. His hound sat staring, holding quiet.

Jonah waved back.

The man made his way around the small pond and approached with his gun held by the barrel, and the butt of it resting on his large shoulder.

"Well, good mornin', suh," he said. His southern accent was thick.

"Good morning," Jonah replied with a disarming smile. "Get you a rabbit, did ya?"

"Laws, yes, suh. A fat one to boot."

The black man and his hound looked over the stranger and put a few things together. Blood on his collar. His person covered in dirt.

"A good church friend of mine, the deputy sheriff, will be along soon to join me an ol Tick here…"

"I understand. No need to be alarmed, just a drifter drifting," jonah said with a disarming smile. He bent down and shook the jowels of the old tickhound. The dog seemed to like him – which to it's owner was all the proof he needed.

Still, it was just a dumb old dog…

Jonah at that moment was glad he decided to bury the cashbox. The way he figured it, the less folks who knew about it the better – and for their own good. But regardless of how he moved forward, he needed to find this Deward man.

" I don't smell no breakfast you cooked. You hungry?" the black man asked.

Jonah was starving. He hadnt eaten anything except the two apples and that felt like a week ago.

"I am, good man," Jonah replied, "But I havent anything to cook it in."

"Oh, that's no never mind. I got me a cabin just half a mile away from here. Cmon, mistah."

Jonah shrugged and finished packing up his tent and supplies. He took a very sharp mental note of the location. He looked down at the earth where he had buried the cashbox. The southern end of the pond.

"Name a Zachariah," the black man said, standing tall.

"Jonah," the drifter replied. He wiped his hand on his shirt and held it oit.

Zachariah looked down at it. It wasn't very often people wanted to shake his hand. But he took it anyway.

"Pleased to meet you, Mr. Jonah," Zachariah said. Jonah couldn't quite place his age, but he figured he may be as old as sixty.

"Likewise, Mr. Zachariah."

Zachariah burst out in laughter then.

Jonah wasn't sure what he said that was funny.

"Shake my hand *and* call me mistuh? Laws, Mr. Jonah, you alright. And you look hungry to boot. So?" Zachariah said, holding up the bag with the rabbit.

"Lead the way, Mr. Zachariah," the drifter said, appreciating his discretion.

Zachariah laughed heartily again and went into a story about a golden fish he's been trying to catch.

Jonah walked his horse beside Zachariah and listened to the story about a golden fish that when caught grants the angler a wish.

It was fair to say that the drifter Jonah and Zachariah liked each other from the beginning.

That morning, sheriff Penny stepped out onto the decking of her office porch with a cup of steaming coffee – a routine of hers. The morning had an early spring chill, but was comfortable enough to enjoy without a jacket.

Down and across the way she could see the youngest Simon boy, opening the corral for the days customers.

She could hear Dougy Getty coughing as he slowly awakened and realized where he was.

"Hey, dummy! Get them keys. I served my time now." The Getty could be heard shouting.

Mandle was there behind her, she could feel the planks moan under his weight.

"We letting him go or waiting for his kin to bail him out?" the giant deputy asked. The Getty's words not seeming to bother him, but Penny knew better.

She took a small sip of her coffee and let out an "ahhh." Penny Landon, sheriff of Douglas County, or not, did not take kindly to people making merry of her brothers low-lit wits.

"Well, big bear, I reckon we'll just let his kin come collect him. I'd like a word with someone who has a more sober mind from the Getty Gang."

"Yeah…alright," he said nodding. "I'm gonna go to service then." He lifted his old beat up bible to show he had it – which he always did.

She turned to him, smiling up, "That'll be just fine. You say 'Hello' to the reverend for me."

She held out her foot to him, and Mandle picked up his foot and they clicked boots, and in unison they said, "Cut the shit!"

Mandle giggled like a child and bounded off the porch toward the church.

Cut the shit.

Their late father's favorite phrase for trouble-makers, and currently, Mandle's way of swearing without swearing. He laughed about it every time.

As deputy Mandle made his way down the road, he passed the marshal, who stopped and tipped his hat to the deputy.

Mandle just kept his head down, saying, "Good morning, sir," and never slowed. He never had a welcoming disposition for strangers, Penny knew, but she could tell he didn't like this marshall Bragstone. Something about him bothered her big-little brother. But nor would Mandle be rude – his kindness being why folks felt comfortable taking advantage of him, despite his unnatural size. They all knew Mandle could lift a man over his head and throw him through a wall, but he wouldn't.

The marshal, who wanted a bit of small talk to befriend the giant, simply shrugged and continued on he way toward the sheriff's office.

The marshal and Penny's eyes met as he approached, and as they walked together into the office, she offered him a cup of coffee.

"Please and thank you, ma'am."

Zachariah Freeman was a born slave, but made free at the close of the war. Having worked metal his entire life it seemed the only work he would get once he arrived in the north. And he had troubles there as well, but met some folks that put him on a path. He kept himself as useful as possible, learning to read and write from whomever he could – mostly children until their parents found them out.

But eventually he crossed paths with a tiny white man named Deward. That day Dewards wagon wheel was destroyed and sank into a mid rut. Mother was in the carriage, on their way back from Minneapolis. Zach's brute strength and knowledge of the iron band in which the spokes were damaged was all Deward needed. He hired him immediately.

Zach worked at the mill for about a year, and his work was excellent, but the constant in fighting from the Gettys and others was becoming an unneeded distraction. So Deward called Zach into his office.

Zach thought he was about to be fired, but Deward said that his father had an old cabin he used for hunting on the not-far south of the woods, "more rabbits than trees, my old friend!" Deward said. Zachariah accepted, of course.

Zach moved in to the cabin that weekend and was informed that the cabin was now his home and he could make of it what he wanted. The first thing Zach did was clean it out, and when doing so he found a gold nugget tucked away in one of the drawers. He took this to Deward the following day but Deward simply shrugged and said, "finders keepers!"

Zach never traded it in. He kept it in his pocket always as a good luck token – and the only two people in the world that knew that were Deward himself and Mandle Landon, with whom Zach had become good friends. Zach didn't feel riggt at the white church, though the reverend always told him he was welcome, so Mandle would take church to Zach. And every Sunday they would pray and read together. And then fish and eat what they caught…

After their breakfast, which Jonah needed immensely, the two sat in the small cabin over a half cup of coffee.

He again pulled the last cigarette from his pocket and tucked it into the corner of his mouth, and he stopped.

"Say Mr. Zachariah, would you happen to have a fusee?"

"Naw suh, but you can use the stick from the cooking fire," Zach replied.

Jonah just shook his head and put the cigarette away, not willing to bother with it. Returning them to digesting their rabbit and eggs in quiet.

"You must have one hell of a story, Zachariah," Jonah said after a time, looking around the cabin. There were fishing rods, nets, tools, cabinets. There were even a few books on a small make-shift shelf built onto the windowsill. It seemed he wasn't living in terrible poverty, which surprised Jonah.

Zach just chuckled a bit, "I came here round about ten years ago after the Proclamation. I had me a brother who went to Skidaway, but I didn't see staying down there as an option. I wasn't much of a share cropper, see, my former owner taught me metal, not seeds. So I came up here. It was as far as I could get from those southern boys who felt a certain way."

Always as far as possible.

Jonah could relate to that.

"Turns out," Zach continued, "There are angry white folks all over the country."

"Ain't that the damn truth," Jonah said. Perhaps he had more in common with this man than met the eyes.

"But since I know me some blacksmithin' work, that Mr. Deward, he keeps me in supplies and well fed. And he keeps them Gettys away from me."

The name Deward rang out for Jonah. It was the primary name on the contract. The man whose money he buried just the night before out by the pond.

"What's Mr. Deward's business? Horses?" the drifter pried. He needed more information.

"Naw, suh, he owns that big ol lumber mill, and I make fittings and nails for him. The occasional saw blade too," Zachariah laughed as he went on, "He got people to callin' me the old black smith, not the *blacksmith*. I reckon it's more clever than 'nigga.'"

Jonah chuckled at that and nodded his head, impressed. A freed slave who knew a trade, could read and had a contract with a company worth a hundred thousand dollars? Hell, it occurred to Jonah the drifter that this Zachariah was doing a long shot better than he was. And in that moment it touched his heart, that the drifter went through hell on the field to see these men have this kind of success.

And Jonah envied him for it. A life in which he could settle down and keep things simple. Go out for a hunt or a fish if he felt like it, answering to almost no one.

"I suppose these Gettys are the local trouble-makers?" Jonah asked, realizing a second name was mentioned.

"To say the least, Mr. Jonah."

The drifter also understood that all too well. It seemed every town in America had its bushel of bad apples. Wherever he went, it was only a matter of time before he crossed paths with them. Or even local law, who didn't take kindly to drifters.

"Just Jonah," he said. "And I understand, being a drifter since the war."

"Uh huh" Zachariah said flatly. He knew there was much more to this drifters story.

"I had me a feelin you was a soldier. But, if you don't mind me askin, Mr. Jonah, aint you got a place you callin home you can go to?"

Jonah leaned back in his chair and let the thoughts of home come to him. He had thought about home every day since the war, but something kept him away from that sacred place in his heart.

Something that wouldn't allow him to recall his father's farm with such fondness, for the danger of becoming homesick enough to go there.

It wasn't shame, he knew. He served in the army before the war and when the war came he fought with incredible distinction. Though he did let his morals conflict with his orders at one point, but he didn't regret that. But the cost of it that he carried, those violent memories that often shook him awake at night, he wouldn't associate with home. If he ever went home, it would be as a man who had let go of the terrors of war. A man who return whole and happy – not to hide.

"Yeah, there is a place that is home," he admitted at length. "I've written a few times over the years, and as far as I know my mother is still alive."

"But you cant go just yet, huh?" Zachariah asked quietly. He didn't want to push the man.

"It just seems so far now," Jonah said, as quietly. His eyes seemed to look out to a horizon that was an impossible distance away.

"Is it too far, or has it been too long?"

Jonah let the thought cross over him. But in response he could only shrug. Perhaps uncertain of what the truth really was. He just knew it didn't feel just right yet.

It wasn't nine o'clock yet, when Jonah excused himself and thanked the black smith.

They wished each other well and shook hands again – Zachariah liked that.

Jonah was shown a path to follow that would lead him into the town of New Arbor, just a mile away.

End of the train line.

And they said their farewells.

It was agreed that Jonah would come back for a visit, and maybe bring a bottle of redeye when he did.

Zachariah liked that!

U. W. Deward, who came into the world with dwarfism, had owned and operated the Deward Lumber Company since his father passed away four years earlier. It was expected of him by his mother – who accepted no excuses.

And he despised it.

The constant lawyer lingering, a man named Forsythe, who wore more cologne than any whore employed at the Dragoon Saloon.

The constant back and forth with shipping logistics for the product – all done by mail until this spring, as the Western Union Company was sending telegraph workers – the lines were being set up that very week.

And the seasonal workers. When the men did arrive they kept themselves thick with liquor, which meant he had to deal with at least one fatality a year in the mill. And when they did manage to not lose a hand or die in the mill, they found themselves in what Deward and sheriff Penny referred to as the Iron Inn.

And finally the Getty family with their constant bickering about unfair percentages, regardless of the land-lease contract they signed – which meant even more dealing with Mr. Forsythe. He had agreed to employ some of the younger Getty's though their tenure was short lived. Deward assumed they were sent to him as a manner of punishment by old mother Getty. He never released anyone from their service to him. Perhaps a deduction of pay, but if a Getty no longer showed up it was because he quit, and Deward never complained about it.

Though, despite all of that, he kept to it with dignity and diligence. He was a refined man of wealth and was fair to his workers when he could be. He walked the mill floor every week and spoke to the men, asking what needs they may have. Many were men who travelled far to find work. Some spoke almost no English. Some were former slaves. And though that tension existed, he kept his men in relative order.

But as it were, six months earlier his mother started having fever spells with fits of dizziness and it had worsened over the last several weeks. His poor mother barely able to make it down the stairs without assistance from Henley, their long time butler. Because of this, Dr. Adlard was a regular visitor to the Deward estate, and the Doctor had informed him that he should at last begin making his preparations for her.

Which is why he contacted the president of Western Union to strike up a deal.

He made his way down the grand staircase of their estate that was built just outside of New Arbor on the land they negotiated from the Gettys many years ago. U. W., or Ulysses, had been born a dwarf and stood just over four feet tall. But anyone that ever dealt with the man knew to not let his size fool them. He glowed with confidence as he bumped down the stairs. He wore a brand new suit. U. W. was always seen wearing a suit.

And though today was the day that the settlement would arrive via Pinkerton Detectives, he came down the grand stair with a look of consternation, patting his vest pockets. He had lost his father's silver pocket watch some how and it was doing him a desperate concern.

He thought back over the last few days, remembering that he had it earlier in the week, and none had been in his bedroom other than himself and his serving man Henley. And Henley would never have taken such a trinket without his knowing – even to have it cleaned.

In the grand entrance waited the good Dr. Adlard, arriving just after nine o'clock in the morning for his routine visit with Mrs. Deward, the dwarf's mother. The Doctor held his hand bag of medical supplies and necessities for examining his patient.

But it wasn't the Doctor that Deward first noticed as he came down the stairs.

It was the Doctor's assistant nurse, Perlina Cole. She was a born free black woman, who was ten years Deward's junior. He found her to be the most beautiful woman alive. She had green eyes and soft brown skin, not to mention her gentle spirit when dealing with his mother.

And he was absolutely in love with her.

She wore the powder blue bonnet that he had sent to her just a week earlier. It was only recently that he decided to dote upon her and it pleased him to see that she accepted the gift and wore it now to his home.

When their eyes met it connected them in ways beyond sight and flesh.

Perlina too, had feelings for him, but in their divided worlds it felt almost impossible to act on it in a respectful way. And so they never spent an evening or even a lunch together outside of the Deward estate, which focused on these medical visits.

"Good morning, Dr. Adlard and Miss Cole," the dwarf said as he made the floor. He shook the Doctor's hand, but his eyes never left Perlina.

"Good morning, monsieur Deward…" the Doctor began, his words thick with his French accent. But he could see that Deward's mind was elsewhere.

The Doctor was a romantic himself, and could see love even when it wasn't so obvious. But these two, when in the same room together, were as blatant as the high sun was bright to the Doctor.

"How is the patient this morning, monsieur?"

"Yes, mother is in bed still. Upstairs." Deward replied, barely turning to regard him. When Perlina was there, all the complexities of his day-to-day seemed to evaporate.

The Doctor rolled his eyes, and smirked a bit at their levity, and made his way up the grand stair case.

"You may take your time, Mademoiselle," he sighed over his shoulder.

They stood in silence for a moment, Deward drinking in her presence. Perlina waited patiently for him to speak. Nearly to the edge of awkwardness, but he broke the quiet before etiquette deemed it too long.

"Our board is ready," Deward said, motioning to a chess table set in front of a most impressive fire place. He held out his hand to lead her to her chair.

Miss Cole gave a short curtsy and took his hand. They moved to the table where Deward put her into her chair and adjusted it so that she could comfortably reach her pieces.

And they began.

He always let her move first.

Chess seemed to be something they could do together that brought a playfulness out in both of them. They only walked the edge of being flirtatious, careful not to embarrass the other, but in truth, it was Deward who was the pursuer, and she the pursued.

"How is Mrs. Deward this morning?" she asked, pushing a pawn forward. It seemed that he had missed the question when asked by the Doctor. Not that Deward had any indifference for his mother, never that, but it was Perlina who brought to him an invited sense of distraction.

"It was a restless night. She is very weak," he said, pushing his own piece. "Weaker every day. She barely speaks now, for the pain is so great, and when she does she's taken to cussing."

"Cussing?"

"Yes. Things I've never heard her say, even as a boy." he laughed. Though his laugh faded into a grey face as he looked down at the board.

"Were you not always a charming lumber baron?"

Deward chuckled and though his eyes were set upon the pieces, his thoughts went back in time.

"When I was twelve I took my father's pipe and trying to be a man of sophistication, I accidentally burned down our barn."

Perlina let out a burst of laughter.

The baron smiled at her and let his eyes lay back to the board, "My dog…Regal was his name…he lost much of his fur in that fire. And I lost my eyebrows saving him."

His faced greyed over though and he whispered, "I wish I could save her."

Perlina still smiling, removed her gloves and rested a gentle hand on Deward's to comfort him.

"It will be a mercy, Mr. Deward."

He nodded slowly in agreement. They had spoken about his mother's passing away at great length over their chess games in the past weeks. He knew her suffering was incredible. He had always known her to be strong and he couldn't ask for a finer mother. His youth was not an easy one, given his dwarfism, but his mother and father had always treated him as a man who was born seven feet tall.

But what can prepare a son, any son, for such an inevitable end? Deward was practical, if anything and concluded that all sons watching their mothers fade away arrived at similar revelations.

That it would indeed be a mercy.

She pushed another piece to draw him from his melancholy.

He smiled across at her and nodded again – a beam of acceptance and understanding. And how fortunate he was to find this black pearl on the edge of civilization.

They hadn't been acquainted for more than a few months, but it was enough.

Just then, the butler Henley approached.

"Good morning, Miss Cole," he said politely to her. "No post this morning, I'm afraid, sir." Henley said, with his elongated British accent.

That pulled Deward's mind away from the game and Miss Cole.

"No post?" he asked, on the edge of incredulity. He knew what Henley meant by 'post.' The settlement hadnt arrived as scheduled.

"The evening train seems to have been delayed, Master Ulysses."

The dwarf looked quizzically at his chess partner, who could only offer back a mere shrug.

"Robbed?" Deward asked.

"Delayed is all there is to know at this time, sir."

Deward too shrugged to Henley and thanked him for being notified.

Odd indeed.

And alarming.

"May I offer you or the lady a refreshment, sir?" Henley asked. To this Deward replied by giving his guest an asking look.

"No, but thank you, Mr. Henley," Perlina said.

"I'll have the same," Deward joked.

Henley bowed, then turned on his heel and disappeared down a hall, off to organize the staff for the days routine.

"Strange that the train is delayed," she said, reading his face.

"Quite," he replied. "But no bother, I'm sure there is an explanation." He slid another piece forward. Though in his mind he entered a small session of panic.

Yes, an explanation would be forthcoming.

One way or another.

The game went on for a few more moments and they spoke of the storms and the welcomed arrival of the spring in their short time together.

"Checkmate, Mr. Deward," she said gracefully.

"Wait, wait…" he said, studying the pieces desperately.

She stood slowly, knowing she had him.

Deward came out of his chair as well then and shook her hand, congratulating her victory.

He never won.

Not once.

And he never let her win.

"One of these days, perhaps," she said, giving him a false sense of pity.

"Oh, Im sure of it. If you come down with a fever I'll be sure to win!"

They both laughed, holding each others hand a bit longer than necessary.

"Monsieur Deward!" they heard the doctor call from on top of the stairs. They released each other then, quickly. The doctor's voice was urgent. And demanding.

Something was wrong.

Ulysses and Perlina looked at each other with a shared thought.

Was it time?

Jonah rode into town taking the path that Zachariah had shown him. Up the path along his small cabin, through the New Arbor cemetery – which he noted had many young men's name's who never saw thirty.

His horse walked at a steady pace and as luck would have it, the first business he came upon in town was the first matter of business he needed tending to.

The stable was open, though there was only a boy of fourteen running it. He had a horse's foot up removing a shoe and the shoe was winning their battle of stubbornness.

"No chaps, boy?" Jonah said leaning forward on the saddle horn.

The boy turned on him and looked surprised and embarrassed all at once. The horse's foot came down as he let go and it barely missed the boy's knee.

The boy was indeed not wearing his chaps to shoe the animal.

"Ah hell and deep shit. Don't tell my pa, mister! I'll go attach 'em now." And he scampered off into the large barn. The boy seemed to have an edge of frustration, which the drifter, any drifter, could understand.

Jonah dismounted and waited for the boy, who returned quickly with his chaps on.

"I'm Matty Simon," the boy said.

"Jonah," the drifter replied. "How much to put her up for the day?"

"That'll be one Salmon, mister," the kid said. He spit tobacco into the dirt. He eyed the drifter like a gunfighter might and it truly amused him.

"Here, that's a deal," Jonah said, taking a dollar out of his pocket and handing it over. "And you're secret's safe with me, kid."

This relaxed Matty enough for him to smile a bit and wink as he took the money. He took the horses reigns from Jonah and began walking it toward the stable.

"Where can a fella get a room and a bath in town here, Matty Simon?" he asked, scanning the buildings beyond.

"You just head on down the main thoroughfare there, past the sheriff's office. You're lookin' for the Dragoon Saloon." He said over his shoulder.

At that, a man with grey hair came upon the corral and shouted out Matty's name. Jonah saw the boy quickly pull the tobacco plug from his cheek and nonchalantly toss it into a hay pile.

The drifter smirked to himself, his mind flooded with memories of he himself nipping in to his fathers chaw supply and taking precaution to not be caught with it. The trappings of an only son growing up on a farm.

He walked his way into New Arbor.

Then he heard the train whistle.

Watching from a hundred yards away, Roger Getty pulled the cigarillo from the corner of his mouth and exhaled a steady column of smoke.

"I guess that answers that," he said with a dead calm in his voice.

His brother John who watched with him peered over his shoulder.

"Vogal's dead? You sure? I don't see any saddle bags or a cashbox."

"He don't seem to be in a hurry and he don't seem to be tryin' to hide. Which means Pete is dead," the one-eye Getty said matter-of-factly. Around his brothers, Roger Getty was nothing but calculating and cold.

John snorted and clapped his little brother on the shoulder, "I guess mother was right," he chuckled.

"Which also means he probably buried the money somewhere along that path," Roger continued.

They both fell quiet for a time, churning their thoughts.

Without definite knowledge of the money's location they couldn't act or do anything but follow the drifter and hope that he led them to it eventually. But John had another thought.

"Doesn't that nigger friend of yours live out that way? Maybe he saw something?" John said into his ear, venomously and suggestively.

Roger rolled his shoulder to make John let go of it. As far as John and all the town knew it was no secret that Roger Getty had wanted to kill Zachariah for years, but never had an opportunity – Deward kept too tight an eye on his smithy. He walked off the planked side entry way of their distillery, making his way to his own horse. Mother would need to know these things.

"Give my love to mother," John said sarcastically.

Roger didn't respond.

"Old Zach," John said under his breath as the drifter made his way.

Jonah made his way through town and passed the sheriff's office.

"Good morning," he heard a voice say.

He turned and saw a strong looking man in a black duster, leaned comfortably on the post. The long tail of his duster was tucked behind the pommel of his Peacemaker.

Jonah noticed these things. And he also noticed the U. S. Marshal star emblazoned on the mans lapel.

"Morning, marshal," the drifter said pleasantly. No need to sound nervous, he realized. He knew about the money, but didn't know who he could trust just yet besides this Deward fella. So until he found him, he wouldn't mention the cashbox.

Maybe.

"New in town, are ya?" the marshal asked.

"Yessir, arrived just now."

"Arrived by train, did you?"

"No sir, came up the southern path, that--"

"Ah." The marshal said interrupting him.

Jonah held quiet, waiting to see what he would say.

"Well, come on in, son. We'll go over this train robbery business," he said. His eyes were a steel gaze.

Jonah had no room for play here. And he knew word may have reached the town before he did. He suspected that. And besides, denying it now would be foolish and only make things worse since he told Old Zach that he had been on the train. So he did the only thing he could do.

"Oh yessir, that's fine by me," he said. He turned and walked over to the stairs and made his way to the marshal.

The marshal still eyed him with an icy blue stare, reading him the way a hawk reads a field mouse.

Jonah wasn't intimated by this, but he could tell this marshal was used to people being intimated by it. He lowered his gaze to give the marshal the impression that he was respectful, but compliant.

The marshal side stepped and motioned for the drifter to go inside.

Bragstone closely followed him in, his hand never left the vicinity of his gun.

As his vision transitioned to indoor light, Jonah was greeted by another officer of the law.

And a woman to boot!

He removed his hat and lowered his bag to the ground.

"Good morning, ma'am," he offered.

"How ya do, Mr. Jonah. I'm sheriff Landon," she said, motioning for him to sit down. It took him off guard that she knew his name. He wondered what else they knew.

"Not sure how much help I'll be, sheriff, but I'll tell you everything I remember," Jonah said.

His demeanor was confident, Penny realized. And he had blood on his collar, from what looked like a good skull sapping.

The marshal stood silent, ready to pounce at the sheriff's signal. This was her office after all.

"Well, maybe just start at the beginning and work your way up to now," Penny said.

"Yes'm," Jonah said. "I guess it all started about four days ago in a dirt floor gin-swiller saloon called Red Gretchen's. That's in Chicago."

She looked to the marshal.

"I've heard of it," the marshal said to the sheriff. She looked back to the drifter.

Jonah continued, "It was late. And I mean it was so late that it would make more sense to say it was early, if you follow me."

The sheriff nodded that she did.

"I was playing poker all night and it came down to me and this fella named Vogal. Pete Vogal."

Jonah turned to see if the marshal recognized the name, but got back only a shrug instead.

"Huh, well that surprises me," Jonah said turning back to the sheriff.

"Why?" she asked

"Because this Vogal claimed he killed six people, so I figured he was wanted and dangerous…"

"Is that why you killed him?" the marshal asked quickly.

"Yessir, that's exactly why!" Jonah said, almost laughing. He didn't hesitate in admitting it. He knew if he did they would feel something was off.

The two law officers shared a look and let the drifter continue.

"So I won the game - a large pot, even. And this Vogal claimed I cheated him."

"Did you?" the sheriff asked.

"No, ma'am. He was just drunk and agitated," Jonah admitted. "But that set the pace for what happened next."

"Which was?" the sheriff prodded.

"Well, three days later I'm on a train for this fine burgh and it gets robbed! And who doin' the robbin'? Vogal and all his pals from Gretchen's. So instead of killing me they whacked my head bloody and stole my wad of cash – near seven hundred dollars! That's a lot of money to man of my means, sheriff!"

"A drifting tramp," the marshal said offhand.

It occurred to Penny just then that this marshal took his job a little too seriously. The thought amused her.

"No, sir! I paid for my ticket and I earn my keep however I may. Honest cards, farming, or even – say, is that lumbermill hiring? I met a black fella outside of town, he said them workers come in and-"

"Where did you kill Pete Vogal?" the sheriff asked, interrupting his thought.

"Oh, uh...I reckon about a few miles outside of town. Him and that other one, name of Gavin. I shot them two boys when they drew on me. See, I chased them from the train. Found their camp and demanded my money back. It was justified. Then they started shootin!

So that went down and I got my money back, and I came this way. That's it."

Both law officers stared at him for a moment. Drinking in his every blink, twitch and breath.

And Jonah knew they were reading him, he just had to remain calm.

"Show me your money," the sheriff said after the silence.

"Yes, ma'am," he said, complying. He pulled out his wad of cash and handed it over to her across the desk.

Penny unfolded it and flipped through the bills. She turned them over, inspecting. Then at length, sorted the bills back into a stack and placed them on the desk in front of the drifter.

"Ok, Mr. Jonah you're free to go. Stay out of trouble while you're in my town. If you're interested in lumber work the Deward Company will most likely hire you on. Good day now."

Jonah stood up and collected his cash. He grabbed his bag and his hat and made for the door.

"One last question," the marshal said to his back.

Fuck. Jonah thought.

"Why were you on the train, coming to this town on the edge of civilization?"

Jonah relaxed his shoulders, "As you said marshal, just drifting."

"Who you running from, vagabond?"

Jonah thought for a moment and his response surprised himself a bit.

"Myself, marshal."

The marshal stared at him for a second longer and nodded him away.

But before he left, he slowly walked over to the sheriff's desk and out of his inner pocket he fished out the red garnet ring. He placed it delicately on the desk.

"The woman on the train – the one who sat across from me. She lost this in the robbery. I trust you can get it back to her."

The sheriff nodded.

The marshal scoffed.

Jonah turned on his heel and made straight for the door - almost bowling over John Getty who was just then coming in the other way.

"Steady now, boy!"

"I beg your pardon, sir," Jonah offered.

Fuck. Penny thought.

"You ain't careful you'll be *begging* me for a bullet, son," John whispered to him. He face was now a mere inch from Jonah's and his breath hot on his face.

Jonah, who almost constantly heard the echoes of canon fire and men screaming wanted to laugh in his face. But instead chose a different route. This was a new town and the last one before Indian nations – perhaps he could not have a fight with the locals on the first day. But he certainly took note of the man.

"Yes, sir, I will be, thank you, sir."

"That's enough, John Getty, that man is free to leave," Penny said, her voice on the edge of commanding.

John *Getty,* Jonah caught. The man's breath already had the dander of whiskey and a gaze that would put down a dog. His first Getty encounter wasn't a good one, he realized. Jonah stepped to the side and let him pass.

He then slipped out the door, closing it behind him.

When he was halfway down the stairs he blew out a long sigh of relief and set the hat back upon his head.

John Getty turned to Penny with an incredulous look.

"Who the hell was that and who the hell is this?" he said, throwing a thumb the marshal's way.

"Take it easy, John. Everything is fine," she assured him. She could tell he was already sipping at the sample tap of the distillery. Penny made her way to the far wall where the gun cabinet was and the large ring of iron keys for the cells.

"Marshal August Bragstone," the marshal said, holding out his hand.

"Very good, marshal. John Getty. Never heard of you," John said shaking his hand.

"Out of Kentucky, tracking a wanted man," the marshal said. "This drifter – Jonah – may be him."

"I don't think so. Just a man in the wrong place at the wrong time," Penny said as she unlocked Dougy Getty's cell. The celled Getty had fallen back to sleep.

"What makes you so sure?" the marshal asked.

"His bills. They were all small singles, fives, twenties. Just the kind you have if you take a big poker pot. Some wrinkled, some not. Nothing to suggest it came out of a payroll cashbox. So his story checks out. Got no evidence to think otherwise," she said with a shrug.

The marshal decided to let it go at that. She had a point, he knew. But where did that leave the man he tracked? He wasn't so sure he trusted this 'Jonah' but he decided to keep quiet for now. This wasn't his town.

After a swift kick to the bed rack from the sheriff, Dougy Getty came to and looked up to see his brother John.

He got to his feet easy enough and they marched for the door.

"You going to tell mother?" Doug asked, a true level of concern in his voice. He didn't want to work the next week at the lumber mill. One of the younger Gettys, Fran, just wrapped up a week of Deward servitude for getting caught stealing a case of wine to share it with his friends, and he said working for the dwarf was hell.

"She don't have time for your nonsense," John assured him.

"She better make time," the sheriff said.

John stooped in his tracks. And slowly turned to her.

"What's that?" he asked.

"I'm going to have a quiet summer, John Getty. You better believe that. I'll build a whole damn prison if I have to keep your family in line."

The marshal was having a pull of his coffee just then and spit-laughed a mouthful. He coughed away the laughter to play it down.

He excused himself, said something about the coffee being too hot and needing to look in to something. He went out the door, closing it behind him, but his outburst of laughter could clearly be heard regardless of the door being shut.

Penny appreciated his response because it gave her confidence in herself, and that he trusted her, but on the other hand it embarrassed the Gettys in an unnecessary way.

John eyed the sheriff with a threat like he never before had.

"You better watch your mouth when your big idiot brother ain't around," Dougy said, coming around his brother.

But John waved him quiet.

"We'll be leaving now," John said with a whisper and a smile. "You be safe, sheriff."

And with that he pushed his brother out the door.

Penny sighed, and simply shook her head and wondered what folks were doing just then on those white sand beaches in Mexico she's read about.

Deward held his mother's hand. Her eyes were closed and her breath was very shallow.

Perlina stood behind him with her hand on his shoulder.

Dr. Adlard was on the opposite side of the bed, remaining quiet and respectful.

"Eunice? God damnit…go find Ulysses," his mother said with barely a whisper, calling out for the dwarf's dead father. In her fever and sickness, she was searching for him.

"I'm here, mother." His voice was firm. He was being strong for her.

Her head lolled to the side toward him. The effort seeming to pain her.

"Tell Ulysses…"

She was slipping away, confusing him for her late husband.

"…to love that nurse."

His voice broke then, "I will," he stammered.

Her eyes opened and glazed over, as if she were looking far beyond the ceiling of her bedroom.

And with that, her last breath eased out with a gentle rasp and her eyes slowly closed forever.

Deward at first was confused, but when her body deflated and eyes shut he realized then that she had slipped away.

With a sob, he tightened on her hand and prayed with his forehead pressed against their tangle of fingers.

Perlina's hand never left his shoulder.

And he noticed that.

Dr. Adlard gently put the smaller end of his stethoscope into his ear and leaned over to listen for her heart beat. He moved the listening end a few times.

Deward looked up to him, already knowing.

"She has passed," he said softly. "You have my most sincere condolences, monsieur Deward."

He nodded his thanks, took a deep breath and stood to his feet.

Deward turned to Perlina who let a single tear roll down her cheek.

He smiled peacefully at her and wiped it away.

"She is at peace now," Perlina said. "God is merciful."

Deward again only nodded warmly. He was grateful she was there to comfort him at the end. And his mother's words were not lost on him.

He reached out and pulled her in.

At first, Perlina thought for an embrace, one of grief and need for comfort.

But instead, he kissed her.

Deeply and with passion.

Her body let go of it's tension and she kissed him back. She wasn't sure it was the right time, but neither of them cared. Not in that moment. Not when their dam had finally released.

The Doctor's eyes went wide and he covered his laugh with a clearing of his throat.

Finally, he thought to himself.

"Monsieur Deward," the Doctor said as their lips came away from each other. "I will take care of all the arrangements with Monsieur Henley, but I need my assistant now, as it were."

Perlina nodded that it would be fine, that everything would be fine. "Let us take care of her. We will be very gentle," she promised.

With a heavy sigh and another look to his mother, he said, "Very well. Can I do anything?"

"No, no, Monsieur, we have her."

He felt perfectly helpless.

Deward excused himself and trusted that the good Doctor and the beautiful Perlina would handle everything. Out in the hall the staff had gathered in silence. It truly touched his heart.

He thanked them and gave them the rest of the day to themselves, assuring them that he would manage himself.

And from this, he was inspired.

He went to the lumber mill and told those men the news. His foremen were most condoling. He made an Announcement that Mrs. Deward had passed away and that work would resume two days later. No pay would be missed.

After this, U.W. Deward did something he rarely ever did.

He made his way toward the Dragoon Saloon to reach a level of drunk that could only be described as most crapulous. He amused himself with his own thoughts wondering if the Iron Inn took reservations.

Jonah walked through the door of the Dragoon Saloon and he was greeted with that old familiar aroma of strong drink soaked into the floor boards. A thin smoke hung about the air, despite it not being past noon yet.

He looked around the large bar room and along the balcony and staircase that connected them.

He noticed a young man, perhaps sixteen years old, leaving an upstairs room, tucking in his shirt – having spent the night with one of the sporting women.

For it being near eleven o'clock in the morning, there was a decent size crowd. A mixture of pleasures happening. No doubt men from the lumber mill had already showed up, going there instead of going home to tell their wives of the granted leave from work that day.

Women, whiskey, cards. A piano played a tune that felt more appropriate for the early hours of the late night, rather than near-noon.

Cards.

It occurred to Jonah the drifter just then that perhaps his life of card mechanics hadn't led him down a perfect path. Even in the last few days he'd been in a robbery, two scrapes and questioned by federal authority.

He decided to wait before joining the card game.

As the young man made his way past the bar, the tender nodded and said, "Young Fran Getty. A pleasant evening was it?" he laughed, his voice thick with Scottish decent.

The young Getty said nothing until he was beaely at the door, turned and said, "my name is Frank, you god damn piss sipper!", then scampered out of the saloon.

The bartender laughed heartily.

Jonah chuckled to himself at the expense of the young man, figuring it was his first time. And took note again of the surname. It seemed he couldn't walk one hundred feet in this town without crossing paths with a Getty.

He then heard a lady singing a soft song about a silver valley. He didn't know the tune and figured it was new, but what captured him was her voice.

She was standing next to the piano, her elbow perched on it as she sang.

Her face was tipped upward and she wore a veil over her eyes. A veil dark enough that Jonah could only see the soft skin of her jaw and the feint red of her lips.

He made his way to the bar, which was only occupied by one other soul. The rest of the patrons were sitting at the various tables.

The man behind the bar was gruff and unshaved. A surly seeming man with fiery red hair, who wiped the bar top to a reflective shine.

"What'll it be, lad?" the man said, his accent thick with the Highlands of Scotland. Jonah was at least a foot taller than this man, his chest barely cresting the bar top, but the drifter noticed his knotted forearms covered with tattoos and fists that looked like they could pugilate a horse to sleep.

"I'd like a room, if you have one, sir," he replied. His eyes drawn to the singing woman.

"Aye, we have rooms," he said. "Were ye lookin fer an overnight, or somethin not as long?"

"I just want a place to sleep for now, Mr…?"

"Errol Brown. Owner, operator," he took Jonah's hand. Mr. Brown's handshake was like holding a stone that could throw *him.*

"Jonah," the drifter replied.

"Well, Jonah, the guest rooms are down the hall there, I'll fetch ye a key."

Jonah nodded and put his back to the bar, yet compelled to watch the veiled woman sing. Her voice was perfectly pitched. And just then he had a flashback from when he was just a boy, of his mother singing while they pulled oranges from the trees in their orchard.

"Oh aye, she's a lovely songbird, ain't she," Mr. Brown said softly to his back. They both watched her in silence for a moment.

"Went blind ten years ago from a fever sickness. No one else would employ her after that. Made her way west eventually. She sang me one song and I took her in," the Scotsman said, endearingly.

"She makes me wish I were a poet," Jonah said with a whisper. "So lovely that it feels familiar."

To this Errol Brown laughed, and clapped him on the shoulder, "Now, now, laddy. Don't go falling in love with whores," he said.

Jonah turned to him with a puzzled look on his face.

"Aye, Miss Lacey Grace is our finest. Which means she's our most expensive, so she don't see many turns," he factually stated. "But many come in to hear her sing, so that's fine by me."

A blind, singing whore. Now Jonah had seen it all, he thought. She truly was beautiful. Her open-back black dress, exposing the cream color of her skin. A color that painters hadn't invented yet. And her naked back, where her angel wings ought to be.

Jonah wasn't sure that he exactly loved her, as the gruff Mr. Brown had suggested, but surely he was impressed by her. To find such treasures on the edge of the world as he had.

Perhaps his card mechanic life hadn't led him to things *all* bad.

He took the key from Mr. Brown and made his way across the bar room to a hallway marked with a sign that said *Guest Rooms.*

He kept his eyes focused on her as he made his way across the saloon.

The drifter made it to his room and after closing the door, dropped his bag into a chair.

He laughed at his own expense having been so taken and so quickly with a soiled dove. Although, he couldn't rightly recall one so charming and talented.

Not long after there was a gentle knocking on his door. He cracked the door just enough to see who was there and it was a woman, no more than twenty. Her breasts spilling out of her dress.

"Can we offer you a bath, sir?" she asked. Her tone was inviting and alluring. This of course was nothing new to Jonah, or anything that would find him subject to her seductions.

He had stayed in many hotels across the years of his drifting, but it was a rare occasion to find himself in the financial obligations of professional women – and that was much closer to his release from the army.

"*Just* a bath," he stated. And just then he looked down at his filthy shirt and trousers, realizing it wasn't only his body that needed a good washing. "And a fresh set of clothes."

The woman seemed a bit disappointed and it appeared as if she would press him for extracurriculars, but after reading his inarguable demeanor she only shrugged and agreed to only a bath.

"And the singing blind woman – is she available for this?"

"You want Lacey to wash you? I don't know if she does that…"

Jonah chuckled at the thought, but let it pass. "I just want her to sing a little while I wash myself."

The young whore rolled her eyes and held out her hand. Jonah peeled a few dollars out and put it into her palm. She nodded and pulled the door closed.

Twenty minutes later he was in a large claw foot bathtub, soaking from the neck down in hot, soapy water. He had a wet rag folded over his eyes, and he heard the light footsteps coming to the door. Steps that shuffled, not stomped. He could tell by the sound of the steps that it was her.

After a delicate knock, the door creaked open and the blind woman glided across the floor. With her hand along the wall, she found the chair in the corner. The drifter could only hear this, but a gentle wind came over him as she passed by and with it the scent of rose water. Her perfume oil filling his nose. He took it in slowly and surely.

She softly cleared her throat and began. There was no music to accompany her, of course, but she kept perfect pitch and the melody was an intended aria.

The drifter had never heard such beautiful singing. He imagined this is what men in suits who wore expensive spectacles called opera.

She sang about how she dreamed of living in marble halls and that knighted men came forth for her hand in love and vows.

Never in his life had Jonah been so relaxed or unguarded. His heart swelled in his chest, but he dare not look at her.

Somehow, by seeing her once and hearing her only twice, this blind woman who had also been pushed to the edge of the civilized world had taken away a bit of rind from the drifter.

U.W. Deward walked into the Dragoon only moments after Jonah slipped into his bath.

The current patrons noticed him and pretended not to stare, but some of them were obvious. This wasn't anything the dwarf let get to him, being the object of such trappings his entire life. He simply waved, recognizing a few faces from the lumber mill floor.

He vaulted into a bar stool and ordered a whiskey from Errol Brown.

"Mr. Deward," the Scotsman said placing the drink in front of him, "What brings ye in so early?"

And to the establishment's owner the truth wasn't that Deward was there early, but at all. He being somewhat of a rarity to be seen in the Dragoon.

The dwarf took the glass and sent the brown water all down his well.

Errol Brown lifted his bushy eyebrows in astonishment. In addition to not seeing the lumber baron in the Dragoon that early or at all, but he never was one to shoot whiskey.

Deward held his glass and looked down into its emptiness.

"My mother passed this morning" he said without looking up.

The barkeep sighed heavily and nodded, completely understanding. Even the grizzled Errol Brown had a mother once.

He took the bottle from the shelf and set it down where the dwarf could reach it.

"No charge today, Mr. Deward, god bless ye," and he moved away to tend to other business.

Deward meant to say thank you, but he was consumed by the weight of the mornings events.

His mother died.

The train is late – what could that mean?

He kissed Perlina Cole…

The dwarf sighed and chuckled to himself as he poured another drink.

Mandle returned from church service and the day was on well after noon.

Penny was just then belting on her gun and putting on a leather vest.

"I'm off to see Old Zach," she said. She reached for a rifle out of the gun cabinet. "You're welcome to join me, if you want to."

Mandle seemed to think about it for a moment, but then shook his head, "I told the reverend I would help him."

"Oh yeah? What's he got you doing now?" She said as she slung the long barrel over her shoulder. She eyed him with a pity that was born of love. Patient and delicate. All their lives.

"Choppin' a little cookin' wood."

Penny let the answer hang in the air for a moment. She knew Mandle helped a lot of people around New Arbor, and she knew that some of those folks perhaps took advantage of his kindness. And his strength.

"Well, you just make sure that if he don't pay you, he at least feeds you, hear?"

Mandle looked at his boots and shrugged, "Just don't seem right, chargin' a man of God."

"Uh huh," she said, looking up at him. Even though they were both into their middle age he still had that boyish face. Behind his beard and brawl scars she could still see his childlike features.

She went for the door, but stopped and turned to him.

He was still looking at his boots, perhaps wondering if he had done something wrong.

She smiled, walked back more slowly and held out her boot for him.

When Jonah returned to his room from his bath, new clothes were waiting for him.

Whores, it turned out, were excellent judges of a man's size.

He dressed and wrapped his gun belt around his waist. He combed his dark hair back and put his hat on.

As Jonah came out from the hallway into the taproom he saw a small crowd gathered at the bar and a dwarf man, dressed in a pin-stripped suit, regaling the men and their dates with a story.

Jonah, yet again had found himself perplexed with the last days. Strange as they were, he wondered what other oddities would he experience.

Perhaps the circus blew in to town? Even this town, so far removed from any others?

It was still early in the day, after all.

He approached the bar and ordered a beer.

The drifter held quiet. Only listening.

The blind singer was no where to be seen and he was hoping to request a melody of her, but the lone piano keyed on quietly.

Just then a man dressed like a fancy butler walked in and beside him was a man Jonah thought looked a shade familiar. When the familiar man put his hands on his hips, his jacket opened and Jonah could see the Pinkerton shield on the breast of his vest.

"Master Ulysses," the butler called out.

The dwarf and his whiskey compatriots all turned to Mr. Henley.

"Uh oh! Im in trouble n-now!" Deward stammered, laughing.

The dwarf hopped off his stool after excusing himself from the small crowd and they dispersed back to their own interests.

"Henley, my good dear friend," Deward said.

"Mr. Deward, I am Captain McGillicuddy," the Pinkerton said.

Deward, Jonah heard. Apparently this dwarf man was the Deward he was looking for, or at least a relative. But by how the butler and the Pinkerton both addressed him with respect, Jonah reasoned that he was the lumber baron disclosed in the contract.

Jonah didn't watch them, but he listened in as best he could over the murmur of the saloon.

"Robbed?!" Deward shouted.

The Pinkertons voice was too low to make out as he nodded and whispered to the dwarf.

The dwarf reached up and grabbed the Pinkerton by his lapels and pulled him down to his eye level, from outside two more Pinkertons entered the bar room to help their captain, but he waved them off.

"What do you mean it was lost? Lost *how?!*" Deward screamed in his face.

He let him go and McGillicuddy stood up tall and straightened his jacket.

"I-I don't think you entirely understand, Mr. Deward," the captain stuttered. "I lost good men!"

"Oh, I understand your outfit probably shit their beds!" the dwarf said.

The captain shifted from one foot to the other, "It's not entirely my fault, sir." By now the room was quiet enough – everyone listening but not seeming to listen.

"Oh? Well, you can *entirely* explain that to the Western Union Company," he laughed. "And explain to your superiors how you lost agents!" He was on his way to drunk, so he laughed hard. Normally he would have taken the news seriously and without outburst.

At the mention of the telegraph company and the Agency, the blood drained from the young captains face.

Jonah watched on, like a stone.

A few of the other Dragoon patrons chuckled to themselves. Thoroughly entertained by the mill owner shouting down a Pinkerton.

Deward was a man of refined taste, as frontier barons went, so this was a new sight for them. He didn't usually take in to cussing or drunkenness, but today had been turning into an exceptional day – for good and quite a bit of bad.

"You're *entirely* fucked, son!" Deward said loudly.

At that, the collective of the room, patrons and whores, Mr. Brown and even Jonah, all burst into laughing.

The Pinkerton captain had nothing left to say. He was embarrassed. Humiliated by this dwarf. Enraged that he had dead men on his hands and that this half-man was ridiculing him to his face about it.

His failure welled up in him like a crashing wave – it just didn't have anywhere to go.

Jonah saw it coming. He saw the look in the defeated captain's eye that debased a man to throwing his fists.

McGillicuddy was a captain of the Pinkerton Detective Agency and their word was law! He didn't have to take this from a dwarf after his men sacrificed their lives to protect his money!

The drifter slipped off his stool and moved in front of Deward as McGillicuddy reached back to throw a blow.

"Ok, captain, ok," Jonah said wrapping him up tight around the shoulders, trying to defuse the brawl before it happened.

The other two Pinkertons jumped in then, prying them apart. Jonah let go only when he knew the captain was out of the dwarf's range, and held his hands up to imply he was no longer aggressing.

The second and third Pinkerton dragged their captain out the door by his arms.

The bar room cheered and laughed as they dragged him out. Deward laughing most of all.

It was on Western Union to hire the protection for the transport of the contract and payment. So Deward wouldn't be held accountable in any further negotiations. But regardless, a pile of money had gone missing, which put more than a wrinkle in his plans for the future.

Wiping those thoughts from his fogged mind he quickly looked up to the back of this stranger who injected on his behalf.

"Ho there, fella!" Deward said spinning Jonah around by his arm. "You drink with me!" There didn't seem to be any room in his tone left for arguing.

After all, this gentleman just saved him from being knuckled in the mouth.

Jonah nodded his thanks and they took their seats next to each other.

"U.W. Deward," the dwarf said holding out his hand. The crowd, dying down went back to their cards and drinks.

Anyone who was paying close attention, would have seen Errol Brown ease the double-barrel shotgun back under the bar counter.

"Jonah," the drifter said, taking his hand and shaking it.

"Mr. Jonah's drinks are on me, my good man, Errol."

"As ye please, sir," the bartender said, moving Jonah's beer mug down from his earlier seat.

Jonah eyed the small man. He knew he was on his way to being drunk, so perhaps it would be best to save any conversation regarding the money. At that, Jonah decided that if this Deward fella was going to provide an evening of intake, who was he to be rude and refuse? Besides, the cashbox wasn't going anywhere, and Jonah was the only one who knew where it was.

Deward took up his glass and clinked it off Jonah's beer mug.

"To my mother, may she rest in peace," the dwarf said. Jonah could hear a slight tremor in his voice, but made no action that would say he noticed.

"To your mother, Mr. Deward," Jonah reciprocated. And they both took a long pull.

"*Ahhh!,*" Deward said. He wasn't much of a drinker and he barely weighed one hundred pounds.

He wasn't quite excessively in the drunk house just yet, Jonah could see, but he was on its front porch.

The drifter ordered him a beer instead of pouring him another whiskey.

Jonah laughed with the lumber baron as he thanked him for the beer.

Jonah scanned the room again for the blind singer - Lacey, Mr. Brown had called her. But he still didn't see her. Or hear her. The lone piano pinged on.

He did see John Getty, the man who threatened him earlier, walk in the door.

Getty didn't see Jonah just yet, perhaps missing him as recognizable having been shaved and bathed. But John was hailed by the men playing cards.

He walked over to them and pulled a billfold out of his breast pocket and laid it on the table before taking a seat.

"Huh," Jonah said to himself. He eyed the Getty man's cash like a hawk. Not that he needed it, but taking it from him would be satisfying. And by the way Zachariah told it, taking a few dollars from this Getty man wouldn't exactly put a hole in his canteen.

"Did you, Mr. Jonah?"

Jonah had missed what the dwarf asked.

"Excuse me, sir. What was that?"

"I say, did you fight in the war?" Deward reiterated, he was trying to take the subject away from his mother.

Jonah let out a sigh. Normally he wouldn't discuss the war, but this Deward man intrigued him, and he felt connected to him by the money buried near Old Zach's pond.

That, and the poor fella's mother just died that morning apparently.

It made Jonah think about his mother for the second time that day, and it made him realize that she's getting old. And one day too would pass. Maybe even soon.

"I did, Mr. Deward. I was wounded at Shiloh. Spent eight months in hospital and then later fought at Gettysburg."

The dwarfs mouth seemed to hang open. Of the common knowledge amongst citizens, particularly wealthy ones, was that those were perhaps the bloodiest battles of the entire conflict.

"My God," Deward said, his voice was sympathetic.

And then his face was alight, "But you survived!"

Jonah nodded his head and took a pull of his beer.

"No one walked off those battlefields altogether alive, Mr. Deward," he said in a flat, dreaded tone.

The drifter took another long pull of his beer.

Deward sucked in his teeth, worried that he had stirred up painful memories for his new friend. So he decided, again, to change the subject.

"So, what did you do before the war?" he asked, adding a levity to his voice.

Without missing a beat, a smiling Jonah turned to him and truthfully answered.

"I was stationed at Fort Warren."

Deward, at first was silent. He had a look of slight confusion. Deward had connections in Boston and had been to the coast on occasion. He knew the name of the fort, but knew it to be a prison during the war for Confederate officers and spies.

"Oh, interesting! Dealing with traitors and spies," the dwarf put on with a flourish.

"I was a convict of the prison," Jonah admitted flatly. His disposition was pushing levity, but Deward could see in his eyes a distant pain.

It was then that Deward erupted into loud belly laughter.

Jonah couldn't help it.

And he laughed too.

"Why in God's name were you there? I was under the impression you fought for Lincoln's army."

"Oh, yes sir, I was a union soldier, but I joined the army in fifty-eight, before the war was declared. I was out west near Saint Vrain. I was an Indian agent under a Colonel Maddox, who wanted me to betray and kill our Arapahoe scouts. I refused to fight them, and men died. So I was thrown into Warren with Rebel upstarts."

Deward sat quiet for a moment and let the man take a pull of his beer. The way he drank it just then was calm and steady – like a horse that had been broken too far. Jonah didn't focus much on his year in prison, but it was a terrible spell – twice he was beaten near to death by the Confederates jailed with him, and in that winter came very close to freezing to death.

"A time after the war broke out, I was released to fight," he continued, pushing the memories away. "During the second day of Gettysburg I saved another colonel's life, so I suppose they called it even and let me discharge without pay. Ten years after, here I am having a beer with a lumber baron on the edge of civilization."

He lifted his beer to Deward and finished the mug.

"Mr. Jonah, that's one hell of a story," the dwarf said at length. He clapped the drifter on the shoulder and ordered him another beer.

Penny rode down the path the Old Zach kept to his cabin.

She was curious about this drifter, Jonah. He had mentioned that he met a black man on the outskirts of town – it could only mean Zachariah.

Jonah didn't seem guilty of murder or being involved with the robbery. She dealt with guilty men day in and day out. She's even stood at the gallows and sent men to their ultimate destiny, but as far as this Jonah went, she couldn't quite place it. Something was off about him. And it was even more strange that the marshal arrived just a day before the drifter did. She had too many questions and for now, the only place to hopefully get answers was from Old Zach.

She pulled her horse up to the front of the cabin. Things were quiet. She couldn't hear the signature singing of the anvil as Zachariah worked away at the metal. The forge that usually sizzled with charcoal wasn't burning at all, in fact. She removed a riding glove and held her bare hand over the coals.

Cold.

She walked to the small shed, but saw nothing out of place.

She made her way over to the latrine, calling out his name as she approached.

"Zachariah! It's sheriff Penny."

No answer.

She cracked the door open, but he wasn't inside.

Penny walked onto the front porch of the cabin and saw that one of the windows was broken out, glass laying on the floor planks.

She drew her gun. And cocked it.

She put her hand on the front door handle, it was slightly ajar.

With a single swift push on the handle the door flew in and she leveled her gun.

Nothing.

All she heard were flies.

"Zachariah?"

No answer. She stepped in and let her eyes adjust.

And there was Old Zachariah. Roped to his favorite chair. Covered in blood, his jaw broken, his head broken in on the side. His tongue was hanging out and near bitten all the way through.

Dead. And by her quick glance, was beaten to death.

And there, laying beside him, seemingly stabbed through the neck was his faithful bloodhound.

Also dead.

She examined the area, though there weren't many places for an assailant to hide. She put her head out the door and diligently searched the woods with her eyes.

She was confident that she was alone.

Penny uncocked her gun and slid it back onto her hip.

"You poor, poor man," was all she said. She removed her hat and started looking around in the cabin for evidence. She found a fish cudgel, broken in half and covered with blood – no doubt the murder weapon.

But that was it.

Blood sprayed on the wall and floor. It truly was a grisly scene.

Jonah had blood on his shirt when they questioned him, claiming the robbers sapped his head, and he admitted to being here. But he just didn't seem the murderous type, and why would he willingly place himself at a murder scene if he were guilty? Could she be wrong? The marshal mentioned that this Dade was a clever one. She would be sure to ask him.

She very gently ran her hands over the pants pocket and shirt pocket of the dead blacksmith. She knew that Zach always carried with him a gold nugget that Deward had given him as a token of their friendship – Mandle told her about it one day. But now it seemed the nugget was gone. Most likely taken by the murderer. But not many people knew that old Zach had such a prize possession.

Mandle would be heart broken, she realized. She was heart broken. Deward would be as well. Everyone loved Old Zach.

Well, not everyone…

"Roger Getty?" she said to herself, spitting. She knew better than to lose herself.

Though, she had no evidence to suspect that Getty was involved at all. The fact was, the drifter seemed more likely a suspect.

The sheriff backed out of the house and made it onto her horse. She would go see the reverend first and have him handle the arrangements for Old Zach. Zachariah would've liked it that way.

And then she was off to find this drifter. He was the only real suspect, but it couldn't hurt to question Roger.

She needed to find that gold. Whoever had the gold was the killer – or at least recently traded with him.

Jonah and Deward continued drinking well on until supper time. The crowd of the Dragoon grew and more and more women came down from upstairs, ready to work the night.

The drifter could see that the dwarf was assuredly full of liquor by now, and they had been over in detail Deward's love for his dear departed mother. And they spoke of the war and the affects of the country since then. Both seeing it from a very different perspective, one being a card-sharking drifter, the other a lumber baron.

But it was time to eat and everyone in the bar room could smell the thick stew that was nearly ready.

Jonah helped Deward to a table and set a bowl of the stew in front of him. Errol Brown waved the fee, of course.

The dwarf looked up at Jonah and smiled broadly and thanked him for being his friend.

"It ain't no worry, U.W.," he said, calling him by his initials as the dwarf had insisted.

The lumber baron dove into his bowl. He was quite hungry, and drunk.

Jonah turned an eye to the card game that the Getty and friends were having.

"You go on, Mr. Jonah, take them for all they have," Deward said encouraging him.

"You're certain, I wouldn't think it right to let you eat alone tonight," the drifter said.

Deward was touched by the sentiment, but looking over at John Getty and having a general distaste for the man and his thorn of a family, the dwarf looked up at the drifter through bloodshot eyes and simply said, "Kick his ass."

Jonah chuckled, and determined, walked over to their table and flopped his stack – not all of it, of course – at an empty chair.

"Mind if I buy in, gentlemen?" he asked.

John Getty shuffled the cards, but never took his eyes away from Jonah's.

"By all means, boy," John Getty said.

And he began flicking out the cards face down to each of the players.

Jonah sat down and put in his ante. And just then he saw her, Lacey, come gliding down the stairs, her gloved hand slipping down the handrail, guiding her. She was a vision to him, but he kept his face chiseled of stone.

Her face, it almost seemed, to be looking at him, her jaw held high and her exposed neck strong and sensually powdered.

A man, likely a worker of the mill, had placed his hat on one of the last stairs, his table close to it and his back to the railing. Not intentionally to fumble her, of course, but in his stupor of indulgence didn't have the mind to consider blind women making their way about the saloon.

Jonah opened his mouth and turned his shoulders toward her, nearly issuing a warning…

But this Lacey, as she came down upon the stair with the hat, sent her foot around the hat that would have tripped her and continued on her way feeling along the wall toward the piano.

And as she turned, her face kept for just a moment toward Jonah's.

Curious, Jonah thought to himself. With just his eyes he surveyed the room and no one seemed to notice what he *thought* he had. She was invisible to them all – just a blind whore who would supply the background music for their evening.

Invisible. Jonah knew precisely how that felt. And thus he again felt more curious about her and a thought led to his mother and family – where had the years gone? It was easy to hide when no one was looking for you, he realized. Especially one's self.

"…probably voted for Grant," John Getty quipped, to which his compatriots laughed at Jonah's expense. Distracted, by the blind singer, Jonah didn't quite catch the remark, only the following mirth. "Might be asking Piano Pat to play something a little…*Ethiopian*."

The others at the table had an even more hearty outburst at Jonah's expense, but when he sat for a game, he set himself into a heightened sense of attention.

Jonah smiled, kept his head down and focused on the deal – a man who cheats could easily spot a cheater, and by the way this John Getty man was snapping the rim of the deck Jonah knew right away to watch him close.

With his back to the door, something he almost never did, believing his greatest threat was sitting across from him, Jonah didn't notice the marshal walk through the entry and take a seat along the wall. In the shadows of the room, where he could keep his eyes on the drifter's every move.

One of the barmaids approached the marshal, "Whiskey, handsome?"

In a low gruff voice, his eyes never leaving the back of the drifter, "Coffee."

Sheriff Penny said her thanks and farewell to the reverend, Mandle still sat in the front pew, his head lowered in heavy sorrow for news of Old Zach being murdered. He held a half consumed glass of milk, most of the first half still attached to the scruff of his upper lip.

Penny took the shirt of her forearm and wiped the milk mustache away. Mandle didn't seem to mind or notice.

They had decided that Mandle would stay with the reverend and help him with moving the old blacksmiths body – the reverend wouldn't need the deputy's strength, there were plenty of good men who could help with moving Zachariah, but Mandle insisted. Zachariah was probably Mandle's only real friend in the whole world.

And then Penny was off.

Off to question Jonah the drifter. Off to find Roger Getty. Off to see about the missing gold nugget.

The blind woman sang softly as the night moved into a quiet transformation from lively to late. The card game was going strong and Jonah was about even though John Getty was up. Jonah's plan was to let the horse mouth Getty eliminate his friends from the game and then begin counter defrauding him for all he had. Again, not because he needed it, but because of who this Getty was – or represented.

This man was part of a certain type of man that Jonah had come across all of his adult life. In and out of the military. Men of privilege, whose fathers gave them all they had. Men who never knew what hungry really was or had to decide between a meal or medicine. Whose mothers had that look of shame that a man doesn't recognize until he isn't a child anymore.

Or maybe Jonah was a card cheating drifter who had one beer too many.

He never struck himself as a hero and he smirked at himself for that thought.

"You going to deal or just play with yourself all night, boy?" John asked. His speech slightly to a slur now.

The drifter looked up at the man and snapped the cards as he began sending them out to the players.

Johns eyes met with the drifter's then, as the eldest Getty heard the snap. Though it seemed no one else caught it, and that was fine by Getty, who invited the challenge. According to Roge's logic, this drifter had plenty of money to lose at the card table.

Jonah situated the cards in his hand and looked at them.

"So, couldn't help overhear your talk with the half-man," John pressed. Jonah looked over to see that Deward hadn't heard the comment – or appeared not to. "You were wounded at Shiloh?" he laughed to his friends. Getty looked under the table and sniffed, "I smell bullshit, men." The card players and anyone listening in on the game laughed at the drifter.

Jonah kept looking down at his cards, "Yes, sir, cannon fire pounded the orchard and scattered us like the leaves. Broke my leg above and below the knee. Damn near lost it."

"Orchard?" John snorted, "Boy, you're so full of shit it makes sense your eyes are brown!"

Jonah let the roaring laughter of John's jab go on for the minute it lasted. Clearly he was trying to rattle the drifter into doing something foolish. But Jonah simply looked up from his cards then. His eyes colder than his old cell floor.

"I was in the peach orchard at Pittsburg's Landing, Mr. Getty," he said in a grave tone. "I was the one who shot and killed Albert Johnston."

The mirth of the table dissipated then. They all were staring at the drifter.

This man, this *Jonah*, had just claimed to be one of the key men who turned the tide of the entire Civil War.

It was known that the great southern general Albert Johnston was shot and killed by a sharpshooter – but no man ever came forth to make the claim. The South believing that man, a coward, and too afraid to make the claim for the retribution that would follow.

Deward, two tables away, lifted his head and looked over at Jonah – apparently he had been listening in the whole time.

"The hell you say," Getty said in a whisper. Though he wanted to doubt the drifter he could see in his eyes the man's claim couldn't be refuted.

"Easy now, John," one of his card companions said at his side. He could see the boiling rage rearing to come forth.

John Getty bolted up to his feet and from inside of his jacket lapel pocket pulled forth a short barreled gun, the first shot went zipping past his head. But Jonah was moving barely enough to evade the shot – Getty was fast! Jonah thought to himself. Sheriff Penny at that very moment came up to the swinging door of the Dragoon and the bullet struck the door jamb not two feet from her shoulder, splinters of wood pecked at her face.

Out came her revolver.

Out came the marshal's revolver.

The marshal shouted for everyone to hold all fire, but he wasn't heard clearly over the Getty's shot and roar of the crowd.

Getty came forward leveling the barrel to put the next bullet through the drifter's eye but by then Jonah had already drew the bowie blade from the small of his back and surged forward, throwing the table aside.

Getty squeezed again, but the second shot was misdirected as the table end struck Getty's gun hand. The shot went through the crouching drifters hat bill, barely missing him again though – and on the bullet went to strike the wall just between the charging sheriff and marshal.

"God damnit, John! *ERROL!*" the sheriff screamed to the saloon owner.

Jonah then reached back and lunged his blade deep into John Getty's guts.

"NO!" the sheriff screamed even louder.

Getty let out a blood curdling grunt as their bodies collided in the chaos of the fight. The drifter holding Getty up in a hug, not letting go of the blades handle, his other arm wrapped tight around Getty's gun arm, keeping the barrel pointed up.

Then the other guns came out. The other Getty gang guns.

Penny shouted over them. The marshal shouted over them. The Getty men shouted back.

But no one cared.

Jonah knew he was a dead man.

Everyone in the Dragoon was on their feet or running for the door, not to be hit by a stray bullet in the gun battle that was about to fully erupt.

Penny ran up and did the only thing she could think of to save everyone's life.

She sapped the back of Jonah's skull with the butt of her gun.

Down came the drifter and Getty in a legless heap.

The marshal stood beside her and was about to spin his peacemaker away, thinking the situation defused. But marshal Bragstone didn't understand frontier justice as well as the sheriff. He didn't know the Gettys.

"Hand him over!" one of the other Gettys called out. "He's gonna hang for this murder!"

"John Getty ain't dead!" sheriff Penny called out back to the crowd. The crowd all on their feet. Even Deward who was snapped out of his deep drunk by the gun fire at such close range.

The dwarf looked across the room and saw that miss Cole had arrived at some point when he was concentrating on his stew. He smiled at the sight of her, despite bullets whizzing around.

Perlina looked over at her secret love, covering her mouth in worry for him. Terrified a stray bullet would take him from her. But at the moment he was fine, perhaps a bit wobbly at the knees, but unshot.

And sure enough as Penny declared the Getty man still alive John let out a most painful moan, the drifter's blade deep inside of him still.

The Getty's inched forward shouting out and condemning the drifter to his death.

Penny had Jonah by the collar then, dragging his limp body toward the door – the marshals gun out, but up, protecting her authority.

Bragstone wasn't certain they were getting out of there that night. He leveled his arm then and put the barrel of his fancy gun right upon the closest man's forehead. And he had every intension of squeezing the trigger…

And then, just before the Getty's surged forward to claim their prize…

BOOM!

The room was brought to a sudden stop.

All looked over to see Errol Brown, holding his sawed off street howitzer, the barrel smoking and demanding all their attention. The Scotsman had just fired a round off into the ceiling.

"Enough, God damnit! There wont be any lawlessness in my place and…"

Then a coin hit the bartender on the head and bounced off the bar top.

And then another.

And then a few bills feathered down.

And a thick clunk of a silver watch…

The situation of the drifter and the Getty's and the law seemed to suspend in time as all eyes were simply curious.

It seemed to be…raining money?

They all looked up at the ceiling where the shotgun blasted through to the floorboards above.

And gold! And jewelry and cash trickled down to hit the bar top.

Deward, the first to talk, hopped on to the bar top and walked down a few strides to pick up the silver watch.

"Hey! This is mine!" he said with a laugh. For surely it was his father's missing watch!

And it took a moment, but then all eyes went from the dwarf to the hole and then everyone slowly figured it out.

"Hell, that's under Lacey's room," one of the other sporting women said.

And it was Lacey's room.

The blind singer.

Everyone looked over to her in disbelief. She had many items hidden in her floor boards, as if she had been stealing them for years!

They all looked at her.

Lacey seemed to sense the silence, and let out a long sigh. She leaned over to Piano Pat and asked "Is that what I think it is?"

"Yep."

"Well shit."

Penny cocking her revolver brought the room's attention back to her.

"Lacey, you come here right now," and at that Piano Pat began walking her toward the sheriff to hand her over. "Marshal," Penny continued, "you start dragging the drifter here to a cell," she tossed him a set of keys that would open her office. "I'll take John to the Doc's. DOC!"

"I am here, madam sheriff," the Frenchman physician said standing out of the crowd, Perlina next to him.

"Let's go, Doc," Penny said.

As he and Perlina began making there way to the door Perlina's eyes met with Deward's, who was still on the bar top holding his fathers watch, standing under the beautiful blind whore's room hole. Her eyes went from the watch to his face, and her face ran grey. Sickened even.

Deward didn't understand at first, but he quickly put it together as they were leaving.

Perlina believed that Deward was a customer of the soiled doves of the Dragoon.

"No, no, wait just a damn minute…" Deward began. But Perlina and the Doc made the door and went off into the night with the gutted Getty and the unconscious drifter in tow.

Ulysses Deward felt his heart break as he stood there watching her go.

After the law had gone the Dragoon seemed to disperse. The Getty loyalists disbanded into the night, no doubt to run off to find Roger Getty who was absent from the Dragoon.

Deward slipped down from the bar top and also made his way to the door. His mind was such a torrent of disbelief and worry he didn't even realize the watch had slipped from his fingers and landed on the floor.

"Mr. Deward…" Errol Brown began, but he could see the man wasn't hearing anything but the sound of his own heart breaking like a mirror.

When Deward pushed through the swinging door of the saloon a distant flash of lightning lit up his silhouette.

Errol Brown collected all of the whores treasures for safe keeping – no doubt when word got around certain folks would come asking about missing items.

The marshal locked the near-limp, groaning body of the drifter into a cell and then locked Lacey into the cell next to him. He then turned away to go joinnthe sheriff at the doctor's office. How he wanted to question the drifter wkthout the sheriff there! But as matters were, he couldn't and had to see about the stabbed man.

"Marshal I can explain. You see…" Lacey tried, but Bragstone cut her off with a firm push on the chest to sit her down on the cot.

"Honey, don't speak unless it's to the sheriff or the judge," he told her. "You have a bucket at the end of your cot to the right."

And with that the blind woman was left alone with the drifter in the next cell over. The office door slammed shut and relocked.

Lacey had never been a guest at the Iron Inn. The smell of the cell was unpleasant to her. She wondered how long she would have to be in there and then she wondered what the bucket was for, but it didn't take her very long to figure that out.

Then she started to wonder if she would be hanged.

The blind singer laid her head down on the stained, used pillow and began to cry.

A familiar scent of rose water awakened the drifter and he forced one eye to open. His head ached and throbbed.

"What the hell happened?" he asked himself, rhetorically.

And there she was. Laying in the shadows one cell over.

Not a sobbing cry that mourned her life about to end, but a stifled cry that knew better than to make a display of herself. One of accepting. She was a frontier lady after all and would die with as much dignity as she could summon.

Jonah wasn't sure what put them both in a cell, but she was distraught and it put a weight of concern on his heart to see her in such a state.

"You'll be alright, miss," Jonah said quietly. He looked over to see that they were alone.

"Im not so sure," Lacey responded stubbornly through her tears.

Jonah stayed on his cot, sprawled out. His head was spinning something terrible, having taken two good gun saps in as many days. He chuckled to himself, realizing the life of a drifter for the last decade just didn't seem to agree with him.

"What's funny?" Lacey asked.

"Oh," Jonah said rubbing his skull, "just all the years that led me to this moment. I always knew it would end like this if I kept going spending my time in swills with our types. No offense, miss."

"They wont hang you for defending yourself. Or cheating cards or even being a drifter. They're gonna hang you because you stabbed a Getty and they own this town." she made an excellent point that Jonah couldn't argue. He had seen it all over the map.

"Why are you here?" he asked Lacey because he had been unconscious in the Dragoon when the secret of Lacey's horde had been discovered.

She sighed and shrugged, "Mr. Brown doesn't pay too well and singing doesn't earn many turns. I'm a whore, Mr. Jonah. And a thief."

There she said it.

Her voice wasn't even close to breaking now. She came to the terms of her situation well, he realized. Or she was stubborn.

"And a liar," he added.

"I beg your pardon?"

First it struck the drifter that she knew his name, which meant she had asked about him. And secondly he didn't see the harm in letting her know what he now knew. After all, it was just them in the cells.

"I know your secret, is all, miss," he said and in a more quieted voice.

She sat still in the dark as the lamp light sent the shadows of the bars around her.

Jonah stood to his feet and slowly made it to the bars separating them.

Lacey held still.

He stood there staring down at her in the dark. The occasional panel of light would cross her soft neck and jaw – and the path of her silent tears glistened.

"I'll be dead in twenty four hours, Lacey," he said, "I know what it feels like to be invisible. I just want you to know that I see you…"

She turned her head to look up at him.

"…and I know you see me too," he finished.

She stood.

And removed her veil as she walked to meet him, face to face at the bars.

His suspicion confirmed…she could see!

It was the first time she had stared into a mans eyes in many years. It was hard not to look at him. And it was the first time the drifter ever wanted anyone to.

They held there for many moments. Jonah put a hand on the bars between them and she put her hand on his.

Another flash of lightning outside. And the rain began to patter on the roof of the Iron Inn.

All they had was that moment.

Two people who understood each other
, completely with barely any words or time to do so. Their eyes reaching through the dark, between the cell bars, naked of any desperation or the sense of impending death. They were held in that moment and neither knew for how long. But they both knew what welled up inside

of them, that stirred their spirit and shined from their bound eyes.

Jonah knew he would love this woman for the rest of his life. Even for a day. His face came forward and he kissed her.

Lacey heard stories about love her whole life, most of which she concluded with a hardened frontier skepticism. But somehow this beautiful drifter, this beautiful man, was a survivor like her. With her other arm she reached through the bars and pulled him as close to her as she could, daring to hope she had been wrong all those years.

"Please survive this," she whispered harshly into his chest.

Roger Getty entered the house and made the grand stairs in a determined stride. Jane came from her room, hearing him, and met him at the top landing lamp in hand.

"What's the matter?"

"John's at Doc Adlard's," he said as he went past her. "I need you to go check on him."

"Wait – what's happening?"

She decided to follow him to the grand double doors that led into their mothers master chamber.

He took a breath outside the doors. He removed his hat and his eyepatch. By then Jane was by his side. Her quizzical look going unanswered.

Roger knocked on the door and inside they heard Judge the hound issue a subtle, low growl.

"Come on," they heard their old mother beckon.

Roger pushed his way in and Jane followed him. He came to stand at the foot of her bed, she was sat up already, her ancient face highlighted by the yellow light of the reading lamp.

"A very late hour, Roger my son. And Jane is awake too."

"Mother," Roger said, calmly, "John picked a fight with the drifter, who was drunk and cheating him at cards."

"You saw this?"

"No," Roger said shaking his head, "A couple of our men were at the table with them both, saw the whole thing."

The old lady paused and took a shallow breath. While she processed the next move she also gave a look of shame to him. As if to say, *Where were you that your fool brother was left alone?* The old woman shook that thought away and came back to the task at hand.

"Where is the drifter?"

"Mother, John is dying at Doc Adlard's…"

"Where is the God damned drifter?"

Roger grimaced and fought every sensation to scream in her face. But he knew better, so he calmed himself with a few easy breaths. Jane's hand on his shoulder from behind helped.

"The sheriff and the marshal took the drifter into custody. He's in the cell now."

The old woman turned her head and looked out the large windows. The storm outside flash and flooded the town of New Arbor. Her thoughts taking all the avenues of her aged wisdom.

"Go get him," she said at length.

Roger was pleased to hear this. And so was Jane.

"I will, but Doc Adlard may not give him up so…"

"Not your idiot brother. The drifter. Go get the drifter."

"The drifter?" Roger asked incredulously. "He's arrested for stabbing John – possibly to death. I need to go check on John. There's something else…"

"Good," the old woman said, "And while you're there, bail out the drifter and bring him here." She said cooly. "What else?"

"I went to talk to the black smith – Deward's pet," Roger said.

"And?"

"And he was dead when I got there. Beaten to death."

The old woman scoffed and leaned forward to look her son dead in his eye. Her twisted smile sending a sickness in Roger's belly.

"You wouldn't be lying to me, would you Roger Getty? The whole town knows you've wanted to kill that nigger since the day he wandered in."

Roger stared right back at her. His face a hammering of iron. It wasn't true, despite his past. Jane knew it and squeezed his shoulder from behind again.

"He was dead when I got there," he said.

The old woman leaned back against her pillows. She believed him this time.

"Well then," she said intrigued. "it seems someone else got to the black smith first. Was it this drifter covering his tracks?"

Roger could only shrug.

The old woman nodded as her thoughts developed.

"Roger, you stay home, no doubt that sheriff is looking for you if she knows about the dead pet. Jane, you go check on John, find out if he's going to die. Then go bail out the drifter and tell him I'd like a word."

She took up her newspaper again reading by lamp light, letting them both know that the meeting was adjourned.

Without looking up, the old woman said, "Jane dear, before you go fetch your brother Michael and tell him I'd like a word."

When the two siblings didn't move immediately Judge gave another low growl.

Roger spun on his heel and took Jane by the shoulder as he went.

He needed a private word with his sister before they set mothers plan into motion.

John Getty groaned in pain the entire time. The marshal was gentle with him, and set him onto the Doc's surgery table. Perlina hustled about the room lighting every lamp she could.

"Monsieur marshal, strap him, please," Doc Adlard said. He was preparing a cloth mask and dropping the chloroform already.

The marshal strapped John Getty down and backed away, far a way, with his back coming up against the wall. The doctor then put the mask on the patient.

Perlina had the lamps going. And had already begun unspooling the thread that would stitch the gutted Getty.

The marshal couldn't look away. The lights and operating room and the handle of the drifters knife still lodged deep in Getty's abdomen.

He laughed for a moment at the fool Getty for drawing on the drifter, which drew an odd look from the Doc and Miss Cole, but the marshal adjusted his hat in apology and tightened his lip.

Just then the sheriff came in with the colossal deputy.

The last thing John Getty recalled that night was an ungodly searing pain that went all the way through him, and a storm roaring to life.

Seeing that Getty slipped away into a deep dark chemically induced sleep, the Doc nodded to Perlina who put her hands flat on the wounded mans stomach, around the knife. The Doc took hold of the hilt and slowly drew the blade out.

He dropped it in a pan next to the table and started to reach for his sewing necessities.

A few moments after that, Jane Getty walked in, covered in rain.

She looked over and watched the Doc work. She stood next to the sheriff who nodded at her arrival, a woman she had known most of her life.

"He gonna die, Penny?"

"I don't think so, Jane, and there's no reason to think so."

"Where's this drifter then? He cheated my brother and then drove that pig sticker into his guts?" Jane held composure. She wasn't there as a combatant, but as a diplomat. And John had done enough damage to their plans already.

"Actually," the marshal chimed in, "they were cheating each other."

Penny looked at the marshal perplexed, then turned to Jane and said that the drifter was locked up and anyone who harasses her prisoners will also be locked up.

"Go home, Jane. Let the Doc work. In fact, lets all go home and let the Doc work. Miss Perlina,"

"Yes sheriff," the nurse replied but didn't look away from the task of cleaning around the wound so the Doctor could see.

"You let me know if anything changes," Penny instructed.

"Yes ma'am, I certainly will."

With that Penny motioned for the other three to leave the room.

She was the last one to leave and before she did, leaned in close to the French physician and put a gentle hand on his arm, "Do a good job, Doc."

Doc Adlard didn't respond. He kept focused and kept stitching, though sweat was already beginning to bead on his brow. He knew who was on his table and was there to witness the fight. Doc Adlard understood clearly what the sheriff meant – if John Getty dies, all hell will break loose, which meant more bodies on his table.

But the sheriff couldn't help but notice as she walked out that John Getty was the color of freshly made paper.

Out on the porch Jane stopped Penny before she went off into the rain.

"Sheriff I'd like to pay the bail on the drifter called Jonah," she said to Penny's back. This stopped the sheriff in her tracks.

Mandle let out a curious, "Huh now?"

The marshal snorted at the far possibility.

Penny spun on her heel and faced the eldest Getty daughter.

"And why would that be, Jane? Does your mother want a word with my prisoner?"

"Naturally."

"Bail denied," Penny said without letting any air in the discussion.

Jane just stood there, pleasantly. Her hands tucked away in the forward folds of her dress. It wasn't really the sheriffs place to deny any bail or set the bail, for that matter but Jane let this fact go. She was only there for information, really.

"Sheriff," Jane said calmly, "you and I have always been civil with each other. I am not here to complicate your evening. I was sent to check on John and bail out this Jonah, if able. You say there is no bail, then your word is the law."

This relaxed the tension in Penny's shoulders – and took her back a little. Jane being this cooperative and accepting was odd, even for her who the sheriff always assumed was the more level-headed of the siblings. *Why* was Jane being so cooperative? It was true though that of all the Gettys, Jane was probably the one that she liked the most. But even with that in her mind she wouldn't say Jane Getty was her friend. She knew better than to trust a Getty. *Any* Getty.

Penny nodded her approval of Jane's statement. Jane nodded her curtsey and turned away to leave.

"Where is Roger? Why didn't he come check on John?" Penny asked at her back.

Penny didn't for a minute forget that Zachariah was murdered and that Roger Getty, if not this Jonah, was the main suspect.

Jane stopped and turned slowly to the sheriff.

"Sheriff Landon," Jane said, "I can tell you with all respect and honesty, and swear to you on the early days when our fathers actually got along, that Roger had nothing to do with the dead Deward slave."

"Then how does he know the smith is dead?" the marshal chimed in.

Jane looked at the marshal and nodded his point. "Roger went out there for a word with…Zach…and found him dead."

"A word about what?" the marshal asked

Jane could only shrug, "That was between the smith and my brother, I suppose, marshal."

The marshal narrowed his gaze, but let it go.

Penny took a step forward to make sure her point hit home, "You tell Roger that I have questions for him and that if he comes before noon I won't issue a warrant for his arrest."

Again, it wasn't the sheriff's place or power to issue warrants, Jane knew, but things had a way of happening anyway.

"Understood," Jane said with a short bow of her head. "Good evening to you all, now." With that she went off into the dark of the storm.

The marshal, who stood behind the sheriff took his hand off the gun on his hip.

And though the law officials couldn't hear it, as Jane Getty stepped down into the muddy puddles of the thoroughfare, she uncocked the small pistol she held in the forward folds of her dress. She knew Penny Landon her entire life, but the marshal put her on an edge, and Jane was taught hard lessons about trusting anyone outside of her family.

Or in it.

Once Jane was beyond their sound and sight Penny sighed and turned to the marshal and Mandle and said, "Boys, we're gonna have trouble over this. We better get back to the office and keep an eye on the two guests."

"Better load a rifle or two, you think?" the marshal asked. "These frontier folk seem to have a way of handling their own business, it seems."

Penny let the marshals question simmer. It was early spring and this already. The marshal being here at all put her on a heel, and no doubt some of the towns people once they found out a killer was potentially already in their midst. Was this Dade man the marshal was hunting out in the woods or in her cell? Not to mention the train was robbed, and she was sure the drifter had something to do with that, but wasn't sure what just yet.

And Lacey! Stealing from Dragoon patrons and hording it in her floorboards – that actually impressed the sheriff if she was being honest. But still…

Maybe if this Jonah had stabbed a random card player or even a Getty that no one really cared about, like a cousin or in-law. But this was John Getty. The paterfamilias. She was sure this wasn't over and who knew how Mother Getty would react – but it wouldn't be good. Wanting to bail the drifter out was her way of doing it quietly, the sheriff figured – but what now that the quiet way was blocked?

Too many questions with no answers. The sheriff would have to let this unfold naturally and be prepared for the worst.

"Yeah, we better load a rifle, or two."

The other two men followed her into the storm, without question.

If the Gettys came for frontier justice – for the drifter or the blind singer – she would defend them under the law.

Even with her life.

Deward went home for a short time, but found no comfort in the empty halls of the large house. It was too quiet despite the storm raging outside. He stumbled around the foyer and took down a plant and statue. This arose Henley from his chambers. The long time butler coming out with a lamp.

"Master Ulysses? Are you all right, sir?"

Deward found his own feet and across the room, a dying fire still warmed the large fireplace and he could see the chess board there. Where earlier that day he played with Perlina Cole.

He dare not go upstairs and be as drunk as he was near his mothers body. The idea alone turned his stomach and he pushed the thoughts of his recently deceased mother from his mind.

"Not at all, Henley. I am not well at all," he said. He noticed the chess board was still resting in the checkmate she had put to him. Henley hadn't cleared and reset the board yet for next time.

Next time? He scoffed at himself. There wouldn't be a next time! Mother was dead and Perlina thought he was a much lower character than he was. So why would there be a next time?

But U. W. Deward was not a man who easily accepted defeat…

With a huff he swiped a piece from the board and strode through the front doors of the estate.

"Master Ulysses! Please rest for the evening!" Henley called out behind him, but the dwarf would hear nothing of it.

He was off into the storm.

Determined as ever.

Jane made it back home in a short time and after snapping the rain from her hood and cloak returned to the landing where Roger waited.

"John will live, they say, but Roge, he was dangerously pale. I just don't think he'll survive the night. And bail was denied," she whispered to him.

Roger nodded and brought a hand to his chin, thinking. "As we suspected," he said.

"Mother will unleash Hell for this," she said.

Again, Roger nodded.

After a long pause, Jane told him, "You know, Penny suspects you're the one who killed the blacksmith. She said she'll issue a warrant if you're not in by noon tomorrow for questions."

Roger snorted, accepting the news for what it was. He and the blacksmith never got along in the few times they actually crossed paths, and the seeds of rumor grew that Roger Getty wanted old Zach dead out of pure petulance.

Which wasn't the case at all.

Roger didn't care for freed slaves, that much was established, but his attitude toward Zachariah, and all other men of color, was indifference. He didn't even think of him as a man, if he ever thought of him at all.

He went out to question the old black smith about the drifter, and that may have come with serious threats, but Roger had no intension of killing Zachariah Freeman.

Someone else saw to that.

Mother Getty received the news in stride. She shrugged and chuckled when told bail was denied. The sound of her laughter was unsettling to her children, and how her black teeth glistened like wet fossils.

"Take this to judge Washburn. Tell him I said the drifter needs to go free – the Getty boys, who were there, say it was self defense."

She threw a small packet to Roger. He opened it and saw inside a fold of cash.

He looked up at her skeptically, "But it *was* self defense. Why bribe Washburn if the truth is good enough?"

The old woman stared deep into Roger's one good eye for a lasting moment. He knew he was about to be chastised.

"Because he is a corrupt son of a bitch and we don't know who else is out there working against us, or if they found the money. And after years of bribes from us, he expects it."

"Once the drifter goes free, follow him. Patiently follow him. It won't be long before he goes back for the money or makes a run for it. And mind your ass because if it wasn't this drifter that killed the blacksmith it means someone else is definitely out there."

Jane looked at Roger. She agreed with mother on this – that he should take every precaution when dealing with this drifter.

The old woman shakingly took a sip from her china cup.

"Now go and do your duty for this family," she said. And it was her final tone.

Judge growled at mother's lap.

God, how he hated that dog.

Penny and the marshal walked in and set their sopping overcoats on the hooks. On their way to the office she sent Mandle to see the reverend about Zachariah's burial arrangements – she found it better to not have him around when she questioned her detainees.

She and Bragstone both looked over and saw the two celled criminals holding each other through the bars.

Lacey let go of Jonah and walked to face the light of the lamp. She took the bars into her hands and set her eyes to the sheriff.

"Penny Landon," she said. "Come on over here."

Penny nearly popped with laughter as her feet carried her to Lacey. Was she *looking* at me? The sheriff thought. The marshal subconsciously eased his hand to the pearl handle of his gun.

Penny stayed beyond arms reach as she approached the jailed whore, of course. The sheriff wasn't a fool and her father trained her way too well.

"Well then," Penny said shrugging.

The marshals eyes darted from the alleged blind whore to the sheriff and back again. His senses gone in to that other place of instinct – ready to draw and fire in the same fluid motion.

He kept a tight eye on the drifter too. If this man claiming to be called Jonah even twitched a muscle he would put lead in his knee.

"Sheriff I can see," Lacey said flatly.

"Well, praise the lord, it's a miracle," Penny chuckled. "How long?"

"The whole time," she replied. "I was never blind, but I knew a lady in Pittsburgh who was and I learned it from her. How to act the part n'all."

Penny nodded and let the information process and sink in for a moment as she stared Lacey in the eyes. Eyes she had never seen before because Lacey always wore a veil that covered them.

"Does Errol know? Was the stealing his idea?"

"Of course not, sheriff. Errol Brown is a kind man."

"And you mistook that for weakness," Penny said her tone becoming Annoyed at the conversation.

"Sheriff, I –"

But after that, Penny shrugged again, "I honestly don't care. You're a whore who stole money from the hard working men of this town. Judge Washburn will decide if you're worth a trial, Lacey – if that's even your real name."

Lacey fought an outburst of tears and simply lowered her head.

The sheriff's harsh words, though they may have been true, made Jonah feel a certain way.

Penny side-stepped and aligned herself with Jonah's cell.

"And speaking of false names," the marshal said coming to stand beside the sheriff. His demeanor locked on the drifter. His hand still ready to draw.

Penny threw the marshal a side glance, but kept her focus on the drifter.

Jonah noticed this and let it pass without reaction.

"She's just a survivor, making her way in the world, sheriff. And how could she spend it?" Jonah said in Lacey's defense. He turned and faced her.

This touched the green-eyed Lacey.

"Keep your hands up on them bars, drifter," Penny said. "You move one finger, and-" she looked over her shoulder.

The marshal didn't draw his gun, but his clicked the hammer back and stared the drifter dead in his eye.

Penny reached out and put her hand in Jonah's shirt pocket.

Nothing in there but a bent up cigarette.

"Would you happen to have a fusee?" the drifter asked her, smirking.

The sheriff answered his question with a skeptical smirk and stuffed the cigarette back into his shirt pocket.

She then put her hand in his front trouser pocket.

Her face turned a dour color.

Jonah's eyebrow lifted as he felt the sheriff take hold of an object.

Penny pulled forth a small nugget of California gold.

Zachariah Freeman's gold.

She held the nugget up to let its vibrant yellow reflect of the lamp light.

"What in the fuck is that?" Jonah asked.

U. W. fought his way through the dark and flashes of storm, but he knew this town almost as well as anyone. He came to a very dark alley and silently went to the door there. It had a sign that said to please use the front entrance.

He knuckled the old brass knob and rattled it.

Locked.

He knocked.

No response. He adjusted the broad collar of his coat to better protect his neck and face from the torrential rain.

He knocked again.

And then he could see a light coming. A candle through the blurry pane of green glass. Perhaps he hadn't thought this through, but he didn't care. He needed to see her.

The door opened and he was face to face with Perlina Cole.

He looked up at her face, softened by the candle she carried. She looked at him, not knowing what to do, or if she even had the time, a patient was dying.

A patient under her care.

"Mr. Deward…" she said. Her voice insisted an urgency.

She could see that the formal use of his name hurt him in an unfamiliar way. And even though it was pouring rain, she could see he was crying.

"I would never…" he tried to say.

She straightened herself with dignity.

He came forward and put a single item in her hand. He dare not kiss her. He dare not touch her, but to hold her hand as he place the item into it. His eyes ached for her to believe him.

Perlina wanted to speak, but Deward turned and vanished into the storm.

She came forward into the rain, wanting to call out to him, not wanting him to go. But he was already beyond her voice. The storm was too much. Any thought of John Getty dying on the table fled her as quickly as the lightning flashed.

She looked down into her palm and her lips trembled at what lay there. And she knew she loved him. Her other hand went to her heart and then to her lips.

And the tears came and fell into her palm onto the item.

The black queen.

Roger and Jane were far down the hall in his room, away from prying ears and eyes.

"Something isn't right," Roger said to her. He stood in front of a large window as the storm flash and flooded outside. There were sounds throughout the house.

Movement.

Jane sat on the bed behind him, quietly. She had never seen him like this, but only twice. And that was many years ago when his sons died. His heart thrown into despair and indifference. It was when he left the north and went south to hunt runaway slaves. And took to heavy drinking. He became a man of severe brutality. But, when he learned that Janes's daughter died of a brain fever, her only daughter, he rushed home to comfort her. To spare her the pain of losing herself in the hell of whiskey and war. So he came home to her. Consoled her and in that healed some of his own wounds as well. Though mother Getty had already set his heart's scars to her use. By then Roger Getty had become the face of Getty vengeance. By now, when the town saw Roger Getty coming, they moved and gave him birth of the street. His mothers influence and gossip poisoning the truth.

He took a deep and long breath and thought about his life and this family since he came back. And if he was going to be perfectly honest with himself he didn't care about any of them. He didn't care if John died. He didn't care if his mother died. All the other siblings he had nothing in common with or the children or grand children or in-laws…

None but Jane.

He turned to her and leaned against the window sill. Looking at her.

She saw the look in his eye. That pained and exhausted look.

The same look he had when his sons died.

"I'm damn tired of all of this, Janey," Roger said. His voice was weak and near breaking. "And John's going to die and when he does she's going to use it as an excuse to burn this town to the ground hunting down that drifter."

Jane nodded, completely agreeing, "But what do we do? Do we warn Penny? Tell the people we stand apart? How do we get the Deward money before anyone else?"

Roger was shaking his head before she finished her thought.

"We don't," he said flatly. "we just leave. Tonight."

"Leave? And go where? With what money? Isn't the point of all this *money*?"

Roger held up the fold of cash intended to bribe judge Washburn.

"This is a thousand dollars, Jane. We can start another life somewhere. It wont be easy, but we can have our own lives."

Jane went silent.

"If I had to guess," Roger said, "this represents the last of the Getty estate. She wants that money from the Deward deal to push Deward out and buy everything up – even the law. And when she's gone – then what? I don't want to be here to be stabbed in the back by a cousin in a couple years, or to watch it happen to you."

Jane stood up and walked to the window, to stand beside her brother.

Her thoughts went deep into his proposal and she considered leaving her home and everything she knew, all her life. She had never left the Minnesota Territory. She had a husband who left after their daughter died. So he and their daughter were both gone. All she had was her family, and if she was going to be honest with herself, she didn't care about any of them. They were all conniving snakes – from the venerable mother Getty all the way down to the youngest grandchild. Not a single trusting soul to be found.

None but Roger.

And though Roger had done terrible things, she knew him better than that. She knew in his heart that he was better than a violent puppet for their mother. Or a drunken murderer as his reputation proceeded.

And he knew it too.

"Ok, Roge," she said quietly. "Let's leave."

They both looked out at the storm. And in the flashes of light, could see New Arbor below them down through the shallow hills of Douglas County. A fuse had been lit. They didn't have much time to cut out with the bribe money and escape before any of the family were on to their real intensions of fleeing the state.

New Arbor had changed for them at that very moment. It was no longer the hovel of their family's schemes, or the frontier town who warred with Indians or the place of their birth.

At that moment, they looked on to New Arbor with pity.

Set to burn.

"I knew it," the marshal growled. *"He is William Dade."*

"And who the fuck is William Dade?" Jonah asked following up to his earlier question.

Penny stood there looking from the gold nugget to the drifter. She couldn't weigh either. Something was off.

To her, this Jonah just didn't seem the murdering type.

"Sheriff, with all due respect this is now a federal matter. I'd like the judge sent for," the marshal said.

"Yeah?" Jonah asked incredulously

"I have him involved with a train robbery and a trail of bodies," he said, staring the drifter down, yet speaking to the sheriff. "And that's just in your county alone. I've been after this man for over a year. Send for the judge."

"A trail of bodies?" Jonah asked, feeling a bit ignored.

Penny shrugged, "OK, marshal, have it your way. But it's very late and this Dade isn't going anywhere. Not to mention it's a God damn downpour out there."

Marshal looked out the window and back to the sheriff. At length, he nodded and conceded her point.

Penny turned to Jonah and showed the gold piece again – "Where did you get this?"

Jonah looked from the gold to the sheriff. He had been in chains before, he had on a few occasions woke up in a cell after a drunken brawl blossomed from a terrible run of cards.

But murder? He had never been accused of that. He hadn't killed anyone that wasn't trying to kill him first and that wasn't yet far enough away in his mind.

The sheriff put the gold in her pocket and looked the drifter in his eyes.

"Old Zach is dead. Does that-"

Jonah lowered him head and closed his eyes.

A pain washed over him. A sickening dullness in his throat. A hollow scream inside his heart that left him with the hopeless feeling of emptiness.

It felt like killing a man.

"Does that surprise you?" she asked, seeing his reaction to the news.

Marshal stepped up then and pulled Penny back to whisper in her ear, "Careful now. Dade was raised and taught to steal by wandering stage actors. Professional drifters."

Penny nodded to him and gave him a short nod as thanks.

As she came back to the drifter, Jonah raised his head. His eyes were cold and misty.

"I'll only talk to Deward," he said.

"Deward?" Penny asked. "U. W. Deward, the lumber baron?"

"The same."

The marshal chimed in, "He and Deward were quite friendly at the Dragoon earlier. And they had a visit from the Pinkertons."

Penny turned to the marshal, "You're just full of information, aren't you, marshal."

"I'm conducting an investigation, sheriff. I followed the drifter when he came into town. Maybe if you had listened to me…"

Penny scoffed and turned back to the man in the cell.

"Well," she said, "Tomorrow I'll send Mandle to collect Mr. Deward and the magistrate. Should be an interesting-" just then the door opened and there stood a drench deputy Mandle, a giant, carrying a limp Deward in his arms like a baby, "-day," Penny finished.

"Found the Slight Man asleep up the road a ways."

Penny came over to inspect Deward. She checked his brow and his neck. She gently pushed on his chest and the unconscious Deward unleashed a chortle of a snore. She looked to Jonah to see his reaction. The drifter peered on, also scanning the dwarf for injury.

"He's just drunk," Penny said. "Set him up on the cot, please."

Mandle effortlessly took the dwarf man and placed him on the spare cot.

"Marshal, we can continue this in the morning. I'll have the coffee on at dawn," the sheriff said. The marshal seemed reluctant to leave this prisoner after chasing him halfway across the country for over a year, but conceded. He put on his duster and went off into the storm toward his hotel room.

Penny turned to the two jailed and pointed to their cots. "Not another word from you two," she ordered. Jonah collapsed on his cot, but his eyes never left Lacey. His thoughts focused on Zachariah and how he may have contributed to the man's death.

Lacey sat on her cot and gently rested her head on the dingy pillow. Wondering if she had seen her last sunset.

Deward snored away.

The sheriff and deputy said good night then. Mandle was to head home and turn down, the sheriff told him she would stay there for the night.

Before he left, they clicked boot heels and said, "Cut the shit."

The early morning.

As the sky comes out of its darkest shades to the softness of blue. When the last of the stars retract back into the unseen and the moon flees from the coming sun.

Roger and Jane Getty stuff their necessities into their saddle bags. Quietly in the stable, they are the only two awake about the Getty estate.

"Do you really think mother will unleash the boys on the town? She's been talking about it for years, but I always thought it was bullshit."

Roger sighed and nodded. With the amount of money in that cashbox, yes. She would kill everyone she had to and cover it up by calling it an Indian raid.

"These people don't have much time. Once she learns that were gone and Washburn cant be bribed, shell send them to get the drifter and kill anyone in the way. Our family's future is ash."

Jane took it all in again. The end of an era of corruption and violence. Unless of course the Gettys pulled it off, but Roger doubted it. She trusted him and his judgement has always been sound. In this, win or lose, their family had no real future.

They continued to wrap small items and pit them into the folds of their saddles.

"What about Tennessee?" she whispered.

Roger shrugged. It didn't matter to him, as he had told her several times already.

"You know," he said with a teasing calm, "if you go far enough south, it don't snow in the winter time."

She turned and looked at him, and he turned and looked at her.

Jane looked on the verge of exploding with laughter. Who ever dreamed of a winter without barricading the windows and doors and chopping endless piles of firewood just to survive?

She laughed, but tried to stay quiet.

The smile on Roger's face vanished and his eye glared just over Jane's shoulder.

There was young Lily Ann. Hiding in the shadow of their single lamp light. A complete look of terror on her face.

She had heard it all.

Every word.

Roger turned to square off with the girl. He gently raised his hand, but Lilly Ann was so afraid of him. All the stories, the killings and his dreaded single eye.

Jane turned and said, "Lily Ann, honey, now you just wait a minute."

But the girl was overwhelmed. With what she heard about a war coming to New Arbor and their family causing it. And these two sneaking off.

Lily Ann had never felt so in danger in all of her life. And as a great grandchild of the old mother Getty she was trained from birth to do one thing when she heard news within the stable.

Run to mother Getty.

So Lily Ann took a step back and slowly started to turn away.

"She's gonna bolt," Roger said from the corner of his mouth. He consciously kept his hand away from his gun, for clearly he could see this girl was frightened half to death already.

"Lily Ann," Jane said firmly. Trying to draw the girls attention to her with authority.

But Lily Ann took off like a wild mare. Full speed and out the barn in no seconds flat.

Jane and Roger looked at each other. They could run her down, but then what? There was nothing else to do now. The secret was as good as out and they surely couldn't talk their way out of it now. Not with what Lily Ann had heard.

They both threw their legs over their horse and were on the south trail just two minutes later.

They did not flee in haste but kept steady and alert. If mother sent anyone after them, Roger Getty could not be ambushed in his own land.

He, who knew it better than anyone.

Marshal Bragstone woke that day just before dawn. He meticulously polished his gun and thought heavily while doing it.

He wasn't sure what would happen that day, but he would take it in stride and do what he had to do.

He slid the long silver pistol into its seat on his hip, threw his duster on and made his way up to the sheriff's office.

As he walked through the small town of New Arbor in the early dawn it felt especially quiet to him.

The calm before the storm.

Lily Ann huffed at the door. She had just knocked on it and Judge barked. Though it wasn't loud barking, it was loud enough to alert the wise old woman inside.

The girl had forgotten about the dog and was suddenly afraid of the door being opened. She kept looking over she shoulder and down the hallway, expecting at any moment uncle Roger to breach the stairs and strangle her to death – the last thing she'd see is that dreaded single cold eye.

But Roger never came.

The dog stopped barking and the door slowly opened a moment later.

And there was grandmother. Cane in hand and thick shawl wrapped about her.

Lily Ann slipped into her arms, safe at last!

"Oh, child, child," mother Getty said gently with a laugh. "what's gotten you so upset? Come in, come in…"

Lily Ann was barely catching her breath. Mother Getty sat down in a comfortable chair and rested her cane beside her. Lily Ann sat at the chair next to her as was their custom. In between them was a glass covered dish, inside a few wrapped candies. Lily Ann after a deep breath was calming and looked down at the dish.

Mother Getty noticed this and smirked to her. "Go 'head, I won't tell your ma," she said lifting the lid away.

Lily Ann knew better than to eat a wrapped candy before her breakfast, but if grandmother said it was ok, then it was like permission from God to sin.

Mother Getty watched as the child ate her candy and regulated herself into calm. She watched her become safe in her mind.

And then Lily Ann told her what she heard in the stable. She told her everything. That she saw uncle Roge and auntie Jane saddling horses and stealing money that was for the magistrate. That they were going to Tennessee. And that she was scared about people hurting their family and she was scared uncle John would die and it would make people mad. The girl was in tears.

Mother Gettys knuckles whitened over the top of her cane.

"You are such a good girl, Lily Ann. You have always been my favorite grandchild," mother Getty told her.

To this Lily Ann beamed and wiped her tears away. She swelled with pride. A blessing from grandmother was a trophy of sorts within the Getty estate.

"You did good telling me these things," she followed. "I'd like you to help me now."

"Anything, grandmother," Lily Ann said.

"I'd like you to go and wake up your uncles and tell them to come see me right now," she said. Her voice was calm.

"Umm…which ones?" the girl asked.

"All of them, dear."

Lily Ann hopped up out of the chair and gave grandmother another tight hug, truly proud of herself for helping her family.

Grandmother held her out at arms length and motioned with a smile to the wrapped candies again.

Lily Ann beamed and scooped up a handful of them and then shuffled out the door to wake up ever uncle she had that was still in the house. Grandmother laughed pleasantly as the girl took the treats and left. But as soon as Lily Ann was gone, so was the old woman's pleasantness.

Then mother Getty caned her way across her luxurious bedroom to look out the window.

The sun was just cresting out to the east and down to her right she could see the tips of the buildings of New Arbor.

"God damn you all to hell."

Perlina Cole was standing on a beach looking out over an ocean. It was impossibly blue. She had never imagined how blue something other than the sky could be.

The waves below her rolled over in the breeze as they crashed with a rumble into the rocks down along the beach on either side of her. The surf rolling up as soft foam to tickle her toes with the chill of the Pacific.

Next to her saw Mr. Deward. His hair was combed to the side. He sat on a horse and enjoyed the view with her.

"I told you," he said.

She looked up at him and put a hand on his thigh.

"Checkmate," she said.

Perlina was torn from the beach and dragged back to reality by the front door of Doc Adlard's office being kicked in. And not just kicked in but kicked so violently that it nearly broke clean away from the hinges.

Two men charged in. Both had guns. And both were growling like rabid dogs.

"My god!" Perlina shouted, she came up out of the chair she slept in next to the table on which John Getty lay.

The first man backhanded her across the face and returned her to a seated position.

Perlina's head swirled for a moment.

The men began shaking John to wake him up.

Then suddenly a glass vase shattered over the back of the head of the first gunman. He went completely limp and collapsed to the floor.

The second gunman, Bobby Getty, was startled by this but by the time he could collect a thought or a moment to react a gun barrel was at the base of the back of his neck.

Subconsciously he raised his hands and dropped his gun. He knew that it was the Doc who had snuck up on them.

"OK, Doc, we're just here for John," he said trying to control the situation.

"John is dead. He died an hour ago," the Doc said matter-of-factly.

"Alright, it's alright," Bobby said calmly half turning. But went at the Doctor in a rush. They went to the floor in a heap of ripping and flying fists. Fighting over the gun in Doc's hand.

He didn't know what was happening, but it was all wrong. Frontier justice had come to New Arbor, it seemed. He couldn't risk losing this fight and Perlina left alone with this stinking brute.

"Mademoiselle Perlina…*run!*"

She nodded as the scrape continued, getting to her feet she made for the back door. She opened it and thought of going back to help, but as she crossed the threshold she heard a muffled single shot.

And all the racket inside stopped.

Fear overtook her.

She ran for her life down the alley.

Running as fast as she could.

Jonah woke to the gentle clunking of the sheriff making coffee. It wasn't fully dawn yet he could tell, but the sun was breaking.

Lacey and Deward both slept peacefully on their cots.

Jonah stood up and stretched. And walked over to the bars to watch the sheriff.

"I like a small dash of salt in mine," he told her.

Penny chuckled.

And Penny found that she needed a chuckle. She turned to the drifter after she set the water on the stovetop.

"What am I gonna do with you, drifter?" she asked him.

Truly she didn't want to see this man hang later that day, but Washburn wasn't really a listening type. Penny was certain the man took bribes and was going to be paid either way. Since Jane Getty wanted Jonah to ho free maybe he had hope that mother Getty would bribe the judge and set Jonah free? It was the only fighting chance he had really. She couldn't just let him go.

Could she?

Penny Landon wondered then what her father would do.

Jonah wanted to talk it out and he had a thought or two about if this John Getty man lived or died. The way the drifter saw it, was that if Getty died, they would hang him – whether by frontier justice or court order. But if Getty lived, they would send him to prison for a time.

And after his first stretch of time in prison, Jonah preferred that Getty died and he wrap it all up here and now.

He and the sheriff then heard a man shouting outside in the street. And then they heard who sounded like the marshal shouting back, – something about a wanted man? But marshal sounded closer, as if he were on the porch.

There was a distant pop. Like a bottle of champagne being opened a few doors down. The sheriff and drifter looked at each other quizzically.

Then a gunshot rang out and a bullet ripped through the window, striking the wall of posters.

Both Jonah and Penny crouched involuntarily and looked at each other again.

The marshal came in the front door in nearly a crawl, his gun out and up, as more bullets thudded into the walls.

"There's some gentlemen outside that want the drifter cut loose into their custody," he said locking the door.

Then fearlessly and with a pleasant smile, he added, "Good morning – coffee ready?"

They all laughed. There was nothing else to do.

And so it began.

Roger and Jane weren't a mile away when they heard the first shots back in town.

"My god," Jane said. Her voice trembled. She knew it would come to this, but the reality of hearing it play out was something different entirely.

Roger saw how the sound of gunshots affected his sister. And it made him consider how they affected him as well.

And the conclusion he arrived at was such, "Better to hear the bullets than feel them. Come on, let's keep moving."

"Roger...I..." she said, but she lost her voice to a sob.

Roger Getty gave his sister a moment of silence then. He took a long and steady deep breath as they sat on their horses on the south trail. Then moved his horse over to stand beside her and put a hand on her arm.

Not really as comfort, but to get her full attention.

"If we're all lucky, God will forget this damn town ever existed," he said looking hard in her eyes.

Jane knew the truth of it then. She steadied her sobbing with a deep breath and a nod to her brother.

What would she do without him? She wondered just then. She would have probably poisoned herself to death years ago if wasn't for him. And if she stayed today, she would end up dead somehow anyway.

"OK. I'm OK," she said. Her voice was shallow and barely a whisper.

Roger turned his horse and they both continued walking south.

They didn't plan on stopping again until they were in Iowa.

Deward shot up off his cot, "The horse is too big, mother!" the half man grunted as he came out of a dream.

Only to find himself thrown into a nightmare.

"Get down!" Penny shouted back at him. And Deward hit the floor flat. He shouted something to the sheriff but it was drowned out by shattering glass and splinting wood planks.

Lacey was already awake and screaming in terror as bullets riddled the building. Jonah yelling at her to stay on the floor and get under her cot.

The drifter shook the bars violently, "Let me out of here and give me a gun, sheriff!"

To which the marshal laughed.

"You're going to hang with these lawless bastards before sundown, Dade!" he shouted, throwing a volley of bullets back at the Getty gang outside.

Michael Getty, the fourth eldest Getty and newly appointed head of the family, was taking cover in the store front of the distillery. He ordered his men to hold fire.

"Didn't want it to go down this way sheriff. Just want the drifter. Turn him out!"

"Then why the hell did you open fire on my office?" Penny roared.

"That damn marshal shot first!" Michael retorted with equal enthusiasm.

Penny looked over at the marshal who looked back at her, as he reloaded. "They went for their guns," he said with a shrug.

Penny rolled her eyes when the marshal turned away from her to look back at the scene outside.

"Well," Penny said at length, "you can't have the drifter, Michael! He is a lawfully obtained prisoner of the court of Douglas County! And besides, John Getty ain't dead!"

"Hey sheriff!" another man from down the street called out. This being Bobby Getty, who wasn't a sibling but by marriage.

Penny leaned up and looked down the way at him.

Bobby had blood covering the front of himself and he threw an object at the office. An object that landed on the porch. Penny looked out the broken window and down at what it was.

Doc's glasses.

"John and the Doc are both dead!" Bobby said – more to Michael than the sheriff.

"Son of a bitch!" Michael shrilled. Not because he had an affinity for his older brother John, but because the family had been slighted and offended. That someone had killed the eldest son of his mother, whom above all else he aimed to please.

"Fuck." Penny said to herself.

The Gettys opened fire again. And now there were shots coming in at another angle from Bobby Getty.

Just then, there was a banging at the back door of the office, like someone was trying to kick it in.

Frank Getty, fifteen years old, sat at the large table of the kitchen. He rolled the cylinder of gun, a gun he had taken from his father's bureau. A gun he had no permission or reason to have, as far as his father was concerned. He looked down at the empty slots where the bullets would go, spun the cylinder one last time before slapping it home.

He stood and spun the gun over his finger, trying to put it into its holster on his hip.

Frank bumbled the gun and it came away from his grip, thudding onto the floor boards.

A snicker to the side brought his attention away from the gun.

There was Lily Ann, unwrapping a treat from grandmother. He knew it was from grandmother because grandmother was the only one with wrapped candies.

"Don't you have a horse's shit to shovel?" Frank asked her coldly. He didn't appreciate being spied upon or laughed at.

Lily Ann rolled her eyes and put the entire candy in her mouth. The chocolate began to melt almost immediately. She leaned against the door jamb of the kitchen and pulled out another candy to brag.

Another? Frank thought.

"What did you do?" he asked her, his eyes narrowing.

Lily Ann just shrugged and took a breath, the melted chocolate and caramel inside washing her mouth with ecstasy.

Frank reached down, scooped up the gun and was upon her before she could flinch. The gun barrel was against her throat.

"Hey!" she said with a mouthful of candy.

Frank asked the question again.

She chewed a few reps and swallowed the treat, clearing her mouth to speak.

"I helped grandmother, what's the big deal?" she said. "Here, want one? She gave me a bunch."

Frank looked down at the candy and slapped them away.

"HEY!" she said again, this time turning to face him. She didn't care about the gun so much anymore.

Frank threw the hammer of the gun back.

"Alright, alright!" she said. "I saw uncle Roger and aunt Jane leaving. They left before the men went into town."

"They …wait, what?" Frank asked.

"Uncle Roge and Jane left. As in left town. Forever."

"They abandoned us?"

Lily Ann shrugged again. She wasn't sure why they left exactly, but she knew they wanted no part of the Getty family anymore. Grandmother said so.

"So grandmother sent men after them?"

Lily Ann was shaking her head before he finished the question.

"Can't spare the men," she said reiterating grandmother's words to the uncles.

Lily Ann then looked down at the gun, seeing that Frank was off in thought.

"Can I go now?" she asked.

Frank stepped away and nodded. Lily Ann was out the door in a flash, but not before snatching up the candies on the floor.

Frank Getty wasn't invited to go with the men in town.

But he could go get Roger and Jane!

The thoughts of being a hero to his grandmother, doing her such an incredible service…well, he was too old to care about candy.

He went to his father's room. To John Gettys room. He opened the top drawer of the bureau and loaded the gun.

Today he would show them that he wasn't little Fran anymore. That he was Frank Getty. A man to be noticed.

Today he would earn their respect.

"Who's out there?" Penny shouted to the back door.

"Sheriff! It's Perlina Cole! Please help me, let me in!"

"My dear god!" Deward shrilled. He stood amidst the flying bullets and wooden shrapnel pieces. He didn't care. His beloved was outside and in serious danger.

He unlatched the door and opened it for her. They landed in each other's arms on the floor and then scampered back to hide behind the stove.

Penny watched without blinking – despite the bullets being exchanged. What in the hell was happening to her town? She barely recognized it anymore.

Gun battles, secret lovers, blind whores who aren't blind, suspicious drifters!

"HEY!" the marshal shouted, "If you're busy maybe we'll all come back later!" he said as he volleyed half of his cylinder at the Gettys.

Penny snapped back to the task at hand. She looked over at the drifter shouting at her to let him out to help. She saw a look in his eye. A fearlessness in the face of death.

The sheriff, crouched and putting two bullets out the window, shuffled over to her desk and grabbed the iron ring of keys.

"What do you think you're doing?" the marshal asked. He had a level of threat in his tone.

"This is my town, marshal. And I'm not about to watch it burn."

Penny threw the keys to Jonah.

The marshal eyed the drifter with equal threat as he grabbed the keys and started fitting it into the cell lock.

"Marshal!" the sheriff yelled.

The two law officials started shooting. The marshal knew they needed help and this man could save his skin. He made a mental note to not put his back to the drifter and to keep a spare eye on him.

Jonah came flying out of his cell and slid across the floor to slam into the base of the sheriffs gun cabinet.

His gun belt was waiting for him and he slung it over his neck and shoulder.

He then reached up, because the glass was already shattered in the cabinet, and took out the Henry rifle he had taken from the robbery sentry.

And started loading it.

A feeling of dread washed over Jonah. The same feeling he had in the hills out beyond St. Vrains. The same feeling he had at the bugle sound on the battlefield. A terrifying dullness that wiped his mortal senses clean and left only instinct to effectively kill every man who was trying to kill him.

It scared him beyond words. And in that moment he realized that all of the violence he had experienced had broken his heart. And that he wanted to live to see it finished.

Jonah wanted to survive this.

He put the butt of the rifle into his shoulder and levered a round into the chamber.

Jonah the drifter took in a breath and let it out slowly. Time seemed to slow down for him as the focus of battle came.

He didn't approach the window to expose himself, he steadied the rifle right past the marshal's hat, across the room and out beyond. To where he could see the deck of the Getty distillery.

His first shot took Michael Getty just above his nose, where his dirty eyebrows met in a tangle.

The man fell flat onto his back, his eyes contorted for the bullet buried in his brain.

"God and Christ!" the marshal shouted in shock, for the bullet zipped right past his ear on its way to end Michael.

But the drifter didn't hear him. He levered another round as his eyes swept the outer building, seeing a man who had climbed on its roof to get a better angle.

His second shot went through the man's throat, spinning him forward to fall hard onto the street.

A volley came back with rage and outcry for the Getty fallen leader. The men outside screaming curses.

Jonah compacted his frame and shuffled backwards, coming to the stove where he met Deward and Miss Cole, hunkered down.

"Mr. Jonah," Deward greeted him cordially. The drifter could see the man was visibly shaking and had an arm around his woman.

Jonah drew out his volcanic pistol and handed it, grip first, to Deward.

"You'll be fine," he told Deward.

Deward nodded and took the gun.

Perlina Cole whimpered behind the two men.

Jonah looked Deward in the eye then. He leaned in close to the dwarf.

"I have your cashbox. I didn't steal it, but I ended up with it," he said into Deward's ear. And Deward looking back into the man's eye, a man who had just handed him his own gun, believed him.

Deward nodded once to let him know he understood. Perlina whimpered again as bullets were getting close to them – one ricocheting off the stove and into the ceiling.

The dwarf grabbed Jonah by the front of his shirt and pulled him in close, an inch from his face.

"You save this woman's life, Jonah the drifter, and you can keep every dollar."

The drifter nodded once, as the dwarf had, to let him know he understood.

All of his adult life Jonah had been surrounded by violence. Since the day he left his family's farm all those years ago, it's been a string of pain and sorrow. Caused by men who wanted control. Who wanted power.

And these Getty men were no different. Only now, as he looked around the room, he saw something more than himself. He saw Deward and the black nurse, holding each other as Deward used both hands to draw back the hammer of his volcanic. He saw the sheriff and marshal fighting for their lives, shouting at each other. And he saw Lacey. Tears running fast down from her beautiful eyes. Eyes looking up to him for help. To save her.

To survive this.

If those men outside wanted power. If they needed to see violence for their crooked and devilish nature…

Then Benjamin Miguel Jonah was there to give it to them.

He levered his rifle.

The drifter then came out from behind the stove and sent two shots out the window.

Two more Getty men died.

Penny and the marshal kept up as best they could, but they were getting overwhelmed and the men outside were spreading out.

Jonah grabbed a box of shells and backed up toward the rear door that Perlina had come through.

"Where the hell do you think you're going?" the marshal roared. He considered putting a bullet in the man's knee to keep him in place.

"We're getting flanked! I have to get to high ground to slow the spread!" Jonah said over the gun shots.

"Go god damnit!" Penny shouted. She looked at the marshal and said with a shrug, "You can't hang him if you're dead, marshal!"

The marshal let out a grunt of frustration and kept shooting out the window.

He and the sheriff were starting to run out of bullets.

Old mother Getty caned her way to the window of her master bedroom and with shaking and venerable hands, opened the window.

She could hear the gun battle ensuing down in the town. A wry, crooked smile cracked on her face.

She could feel the money in her hands already. It would secure the family well into the next century. Long after she had been gone.

Adjusting the spectacles on her face she saw a lone rider bolting away from the house to the south.

She laughed her dry and throaty laugh.

The old woman turned away from the window then and went to her husband's old chest of drawers, running a boney hand over it.

In the top drawer she looked down at her husband's old sawed-off shotgun. No butt, just a handle.

A pistol of immense punch.

She shakily pulled it out and checked that it still had the old shells loaded in it.

A moment after the drifter slipped away into the alley, Mandle came crouching in through the back door.

"Sissy?" he called out. His voice trembled with fear. The bullets terrifying the large man.

It was a heart-breaking thing for Penny to see, her baby brother, so colossal and strong, rattled to his core.

Mandle didn't even have a gun in his hand. The thought never occurred to him.

"Keep your head down, Big Bear!" the sheriff shouted back.

Just then a bullet zipped off of the very top of the brutes shoulder. It cleanly severed his suspender and left it dangling at his hip.

Mandle went down in a heap. Face down and cowering his head. He looked around for answers.

He cried out to God for help. He prayed hard in his heart as he had always done. Begging the heavenly father to reach down and give him the will to save them all.

And then he saw her.

Lacey the blind whore. Her eyes looking into his as he prayed. Streaming tears and glistening in all of God's restoring miracle power.

To Mandle, Lacey appeared as the Mother Mary weeping at the foot of the cross.

To Mandle Landon, in that moment, the woman was glowing.

He could see with his own eyes that she was seeing him. That she was looking around and that she was blind no more.

"Oh, Mary and Christ!" the marshal called out to the room. "Gatling gun!"

And surely, outside a wagon was being pushed in and a gatling gun was mounted on it.

Where did they even get one of those? Penny thought to herself.

She turned to her brother who was slowly standing up. She looked at everyone in the room with sympathy in her heart.

She knew they were all dead. Even if the drifter shot dead the three men operating the hellish weapon, three more would replace them and continue to rain lead on her office.

Her father's office.

She thought of her father just then and came to a state of acceptance. "I'm sorry, daddy," she whispered to herself.

But still, as she saw her people, apologetic that it would end this way.

The Gettys would win.

But then she heard…

Singing?

"*Jesus loves me this I know*," Mandle began. He rushed passed the marshal and Penny.

The sheriff screamed at him to stop. With all of her might she screamed at him to stop. But he blasted through what was left of the front door at full speed.

The Getty men outside opened fire.

The magazine was loaded into the top of the gatling gun.

Penny Landon watched on in horror.

A bullet struck Mandle in the arm. Then another in the shoulder.

"Jesus loves me this I know!" he roared.

Another bullet struck him in the thigh.

"Kill that son of a bitch!" Bobby Getty ordered his men.

They began cranking the gatling gun.

Mandle's shirt ripped open in a dozen places.

"JESUS LOVES ME THIS I KNOW!" on he charged, unslowed.

Unafraid.

A miracle! God had showed him a miracle!

Mandle in his full charge, lowered his shoulder and came into the gatling guns wagon at full speed.

He roared his song! He roared as bullets tore into his body!

He lifted the entire wagon and pushed the gun and three men over in a crashed, breaking their bones and destroying the gun.

As he collapsed to the ground his smile couldn't have been more wide.

Roger and Jane kept their slow pace and listened to the gun battle as it raged on. They could hear distant screams.

Jane wanted to stop to hear it through, to know the outcome, but Roger kept reminding her that new Arbor is their past and damn every soul there to hell.

And they heard a fast horse approaching. The thought occurred to him that mother had sent an assassin after all.

Roger nodded for Jane to arm herself. And she did. She always had been. Keeping her small pistol in the folds of her dress.

Roger unlatched the holster of his gun, ready to draw if need be.

He would kill a Getty man, any Getty man, to save his sister, he told himself.

And the rider came.

"Fran?" Jane asked incredulously. She didn't feel threatened by the boy, too young and green. "What are you doing out here? What's happening in town?"

Frank Getty didn't want to talk with her, instead, he wordlessly went for his gun.

But as his hand touched the grip, he blinked and Rogers gun was in his hand – very fast. He was looking down its dark barrel.

"Don't do that boy," his uncle Roge said, deathly calm. He cocked the hammer to better make his point. "Don't make me kill you."

"Roger," Jane said like a mother. "Little Fran isn't here to-"

And that was it for Frank Getty. He had been called Little Fran for the last time. It was the last of a thousand, thousand straws that had been thrown on his back all his life.

He pulled and fired off a shot, but Roger fired a half second faster.

Frank's bullet missed Roger.

Roger's bullet did not miss Frank.

A look of shock came over Frank's face. A look Roger had seen on many young men's faces during the war. The realization that you've just been shot and until that very moment thought it an impossible thing.

Frank Getty, barely a man, fell to the side and landed hard on the ground.

Roger sighed heavily. He truly in his heart did not want to do that, but he certainly wasn't about to let the boy harm Jane or himself, or let mother have the last word by sending a runt to do her dirty work.

He had been the runt.

But no more. That was the point of he and Jane fleeing this town and disappearing into history.

Roger turned to apologize to Jane.

And she too had the look of shock.

"No, no…" Roger began. Jane looked down and a bloody hole smoking right where her heart ought to be.

Roger was off his horse and at her side in a single motion. Catching her as she slumped into his arms.

She tried talking but no words came out.

He held her close looking into her eyes. She shook her head, trying to talk.

He leaned in, pressed his ear to her mouth as her words came out, barely a whisper.

"Don't…go back..."

He pulled away and her last breath slipped out. Her eyes gone off to the sky in a wide display of awe at the coming next life.

"Please stay," he heard himself say to her, but he knew better than that. Roger Getty wasn't a man of tears.

But when his sister Jane died in his arms, his dark eye patch went wet with sorrow.

And rage.

Before he knew what he was doing he was on his horse and ripping through the forest trail as fast as he could.

Back to town.

"Nooo!" the sheriff screamed. Her gun roaring along with her.

The marshal's mouth hung open as he wasn't sure he saw what he just saw. He kept firing.

Jonah had just reached the roof of the next building over to see below the massive deputy turn over the gatling gun and then go down with at least two dozen gunshots.

When the deputy came out unarmed, the Getty men gave up their cover to squarely shoot him.

Now they were exposed and the advantage was lost.

The sheriff, the marshal, the drifter and the dwarf all opened fire on the Gettys standing in the street.

The tide had turned.

Getty men dropped dead by the second.

But they also returned fire at the sheriff's office.

A bullet grazed Penny's arm.

Another grazed the marshal's neck.

But neither of them would feel these wounds for many minutes after. In the few seconds, it seemed, after Mandle's charge the street was quiet and dense woth blood and smoke.

Jonah saw Bobby Getty mounting his horse, attempting to flee. He sent two shots after the man but they both missed squarely, having only nicked him in the calf.

The Getty man tore away out of town, toward the large estate on the hill.

The marshal slowly and cautiously came out of the office. The street was full of debris and bodies.

Penny, however, vaulted through the broken window and made her way to Mandle.

On the way, she looked down at her arm and saw that it needed stitching. She nodded to the marshal and pointed to her own neck while looking at his.

He reached up and touched the bullet wound there.

"Damn," he said grinning, "Almost made it through the whole scrape without a scratch!" He pulled a hanky out of his pocket and started winding it into a bandage.

Penny kneeled down at Mandle's body. The marshal stood behind her and removed his hat.

"He, without a doubt, saved our lives," the marshal said.

Penny nodded in agreement, for surely the gatling gun would have brought them down. She pulled the small Bible from his pocket and put it in his hand, laying it over his heart.

Deward and Miss Cole joined the sheriff then. A silence fell over them. The great and powerful Mandle Landon was dead. Died singing to God and saving the people he loved.

This comforted Penny.

And then a horse bolted passed.

They all spun to see the drifter making fast tracks toward the Getty estate. In pursuit of Bobby Getty.

"Go get him," the sheriff said, giving her blessing.

The marshal went for his horse to pursue the drifter, his main suspect for William Dade, but in the storm of gunfire, it must have taken a bullet. It was dead, its head wrenched, still tied to the hitching post.

"I had that horse for three years," he said solemnly. He looked on as the drifter left town around a bend.

He looked to the sheriff and spit on the ground in disagreement. He was angry with her for uncaging the criminal, but he had to admit that things would've gone differently had the drifter not taken up arms with them.

At length he nodded and shrugged, conceding to her decision.

"He better come back," was all he said. And he walked off to inspect the damage to the gatling gun.

Penny appeared to pay him no mind. She went on to sitting with Mandle. She whispered to her baby brother then, lifting his head into her lap, "So brave, Big Bear." She said, using her hand to comb his hair. "You saved us, you really did." She kissed his forehead and lifted her head up to the sky, but kept her eyes softly closed. "God, let him only remember what it was to be a young boy. Take this world away from him and let him play in your house forever," she sniffled through every word. The thought of Zachariah and her father greeting Manle at the Lord's Gates put a warmth over her.

Deward standing by, wiped a tear away from his eye. "Amen," he said. For truly, Mandle sacrificed himself to save them. He looked over and saw his darling and dearest Perlina also mourning the brave deputy. Deward smiled at her and took Perlina by the hand and led her away toward the Doc's. He felt it was best to leave the street as soon as possible, but dared not interrupt the sheriff by walking off disrespectfully as she prayed.

And not for any sense of impending danger from the Gettys, for truly, they were all gone.

But the dwarf was sure that shooting a United States marshal's horse was a crime of some kind.

For in the confusing and closing moments of the gun battle, it was Ulysses W. Deward who secretly put a bullet in the marshal's horse. He didn't want the marshal to be able to chase down his new friend and put him back in his cell after helping to save all their hides.

He wasn't going to let the man who saved the love of his life hang.

Jonah rode up to the house with caution, but speed. Along the way he noticed many townsfolks eyes peeking out closed shutters and curtains. Quite a few nodded to him. One man, motioned to the large house on the hill, indicating to the perusing drifter that he was on the right track.

It seemed the folks of New Arbor gave their blessings as well.

Jonah was careful as the house got closer, any double-backing Bobby Getty did could leave him exposed to a sharpshot.

Always on the move, the drifter slid out of the saddle.

He scoured the ground and saw a few droplets of blood leading away. Toward the barn.

The hunt was on.

He thought of Singing Quiet in that moment.

As he silently crept in to the barn he let his eyes adjust to the dark inside. Flickering shadows from a lone lamp just inside the door resting on a barrel head.

He saw a group of women and children. The rest of the Getty family, hiding from the gunfight. A woman around Jonah's age held a pitchfork in a threatening way, and she would be damned if he let this drifter she's heard so much about come in and hurt her family.

Jonah relaxed, taking the tension out of his body.

"Where is he?" he asked her. His eyes scanned the shadows, looking for the wounded Getty man.

A cocking hammer behind him and a footfall coming his way on some dried hay spun Jonah down and around. Bobby Getty shot first and hit him in his left hand, the bullet also striking the forearm of the rifle, deflecting away from Jonah's face.

Jonah fired from the hip with his rifle. The adrenaline rush allowing the wound to go unregistered.

Once. Lever. Twice.

Bobby Getty fell back, his heart spattered on the barn wall behind him. He was dead before he came crashing down onto the barrel, throwing the lamp down to the side.

The lamp shattered on the floorboards and almost instantly sent a pillar of fire up the barn wall. Dust and hay feeding its urgency to burn.

Jonah winced in pain as the warmth from the fires rush at his face. His left index finger was gone, shot off clean at the first knuckle.

"Everyone out!" the drifter shouted at the children and women. *"Now!"*

He didn't have time for wounds just then. The barn was soon to be engulfed and the drifter didn't want dead women and children on his conscious as well.

As he came out of the barn and the Gettys shuffled out of the fire to safety, he heard a loud tapping. Like glass being rapped.

Jonah looked up to the sound and standing in a large bay window was perhaps the oldest women he had ever seen. Looking down at him. Tapping her cane on the window to get his attention.

She used a crooked and boney finger to summon him up to where she was on the second floor.

Jonah made eye contact with a passing woman, "Which way?" he said motioning to the old woman in the window.

The woman looked up at old mother Getty and Mother Getty nodded that it was ok. The woman said, "Through the kitchen, up the grand stairs. It's the last set of double doors in the hall."

The drifter was off in a cautious run into the kitchen's back door.

In the kitchen, he snapped a towel from a hook and wrapped it around his bleeding hand.

As he went out of the kitchen and into the grand foyer where the stairs were and he levered his last bullet into the firing chamber.

Deward and Perlina went delicately in the front door of the Doctor office. Its fine glass where the Doc's name once was had been shattered in the intrusion.

Perlina saw the dead Getty and sighed heavily. She shook her head at the sheer nonsense of it all.

And for what?

Money? Power?

The concept of such offenses was totally foreign to the nurse of the Frenchman.

"*Aide-moi…*" Perlina heard faintly under a pile of books and papers and a collapsed shelving set. Did she hear it? Or were her hopes antagonizing her ears?

She heard it again, only weaker this time.

Perlina dove into the pile, throwing aside the debris.

"*Docteur!*" Perlina called out. There was Doctor Adlard, covered in blood, but his eyes barely open.

Alive!

Deward came over in a rush to help her with getting him sitting up.

The Doc was wounded badly. Gut shot, by the looks of it. He put a weakened hand over his midriff and said softly to her, "*Obtenez…la balle…*"

"Oh my," Deward said. He was an educated man and spoke French. Perlina also spoke French having been the Doc's nurse for sixteen years.

Perlina nodded to the Doc and the Frenchman, so very pale and weak, started to weep. He saw the dead man next to him.

"No, no, no…" he cried. He had killed a man. He had only intended for the glass vase to knock the man unconscious. And though it was to save Perlina from a terrible fate, it broke his heart. He had taken an oath to save men, not to kill them. But in that despair, he was overwhelmed with shame and blood loss.

His head swooned and he went limp.

Unconscious from pain and grief.

She looked up at Deward then and very seriously into his eyes said, "You're going to help me with the surgery."

Deward was shocked and amazed and terrified all at once with her statement. But he trusted her. He loved her.

"OK…" the dwarf said looking down at all the blood. "What do I do?"

Jonah walked slowly down the hall when he made it to the top of the grand stairs of the Getty estate.

The house was quiet. Not a soul seemed to stir but his own.

The double doors leading to the old woman's room was cracked open, almost inviting him in.

He used the end of the barrel to gently pull the door open.

Inside the old woman sat pleasantly, smiling. Waiting for him. And beside her the biggest and ugliest dog the drifter had ever seen.

Judge issued his customary low growl and the old woman hissed at him to hush now.

Jonah peeked around the corner into the room.

He saw no one else. They were alone.

"Jonah, I presume?" she asked. Her voice was dusty.

The room smelled like old books and candle wax. A lingering perfume attached itself to the fabrics in the decorated room. A large mirror, covered over with dust years ago hung across the from the expanded bay windows.

He looked at the woman with coldness. Something about her looked and sounded out of place. Like she should have died many years ago.

"What do you want?" he asked her.

"The money, of course," she said without missing a beat.

Jonah was taken back by this. And when the old woman saw this reaction from him she laughed a black toothed laugh.

She wasn't laughing at the situation or his reaction, really. She was laughing at him. How he stumbled into her spider's web. It unnerved the drifter. He had never seen a person so old.

"It was our plan from the beginning," she stated. Unafraid of the drifter leaning any information.

"I sent Roger to Chicago two weeks ago when our mail carrier learned that Deward meant to be bought out. It was him that found Pete Vogal and those diseased rats. We didn't anticipate you, however," she laughed. "I should've hired you from the beginning to rob the train!" she said cackling with her gleaming black teeth.

"I buried it," he said, shrugging.

"I know," she confirmed. "But I'm hoping we can come to some kind of arrangement?"

Jonah scoffed and looked her over.

"No chance, witch," he said flatly. And his voice left no room for discussion. He already had Deward's blessing to keep it and all of this woman's soldiery were, as they spoke, attracting crows.

The old woman sighed and shook her head, looking up at him. Truly what a shame it was, she thought. Her grandchildren who have watched the fight from afar have told her already that this drifter was quite a warrior.

"What a shame, Jonah," she said sighing again, "A terrible shame."

From under her blanket rose an object.

The blanket fell off to the side and the double barrel muzzle of her husband's shotgun stared him directly in the face.

How did he miss that!

And then as she raised the gun level she clicked in her cheek and Judge exploded into snarling motion toward him.

One of her arms was a fake arm, meant to look like a gloved hand resting on her lap, hiding her real arm that held the gun.

The old woman's face turned into a wicked growl, her teeth snarling and her eyes going dark.

The shotgun erupted in her hands and Jonah turned as the gun went off.

The man took the scatter shot to the side of his face. And had the shells in the gun not been over ten years old, it surely would have killed him, but the powder had started to decompose.

He went against the wall and slid down to a seated position. His rifle hit the floor and bounced a foot away.

The dog clamped down on his arm, pinning him in a seated position. Jonah subconsciously went for the knife in the small of his back, but when found the sheath empty he recalled it was jammed into John Getty.

She grinned in his face, "Don't worry, I won't miss with the next one."

She used both of her hands to level the gun, ready to unleash the second barrel, careful not to shoot her beloved Judge.

Jonahs's rifle was out of immediate reach.

He took in a breath and waited for the second barrel to hit him full blast or for the dog to find his throat. But her never looked away from those cold and dying woman's eyes.

BOOM!

The old woman's glasses shattered and her eyes crossed as the back of her head sprayed red all over the bay window behind her.

BOOM!

The top of Judge's skull flipped up in the air like a fleshy coin, dropping the beast immediately.

Jonah spared no seconds, grabbed his rifle by the barrel and flew up to his feet. He turned and standing in the door was a man in a black hat and black eye patch. His revolver smoking and leveled at the drifter.

He had Jonah dead to rights.

Roger Getty gave it a good long moment of thought whether he should kill this drifter. The man who derailed their entire plan by taking out the Vogals. The man who likely killed his brother. Who came to be standing in his house.

But Jane was dead. His sons were dead. And he realized that the people he cared about were dead because of his mother and her political games.

But no more.

Roger Getty decided then and there that his mother would be the last person he ever killed.

"Get out of my house, drifter," he said coldly. "We're done."

Jonah stared at the man, another Getty he presumed, for a moment and slowly made his way for the door. When Jonah got into the hall he turned back to say something – maybe something that rounded off an apology for John?

But the man in the eyepatch shook his head and motioned for him to just leave.

He said they were done and that was good enough for the wounded drifter.

So he left.

Marshal Ashley Roberts, sucking on his unlit cigar, rolled into to New Arbor with his deputy, a young man named Michaels.

A fire up on the hill and bodies all about. He saw the sheriff, a woman he knew well and her father before her he knew better still.

He walked up to the grisly scene of the dead strewn about and the sheriff standing over her deputy.

Her brother. Battered with gunshots.

Marshal Roberts and Michaels removed their hats seeing Mandle lying dead.

"Ash?" Penny asked. "That you?" She was exhausted.

"Jesus wept, Penny Landon," marshal Roberts said looking around at the carnage, "What in the name of God happened here?"

Penny had to laugh at what must be going through his head. She looked around too. At the office barely standing it was so full of holes. The gatling gun, smashed apart, surrounded by dead men. The distillery also vented through with bullet holes. Mandle shot with more holes than a fishing net.

"What brings you in, Ash?" she asked, deciding to delay his question.

"Well," he said going with it, "we had us a train robbery a couple nights ago. I've been working with your good friend sheriff Bowers over in Steams County."

Penny couldn't stand the sound of Andy Bowers' voice, but he was a fair lawman.

"Technically the robbery was in his area, so I went to him first. But, we tracked the robbers to a camp not far from here just across the county line. Lost the trail with the dogs due to rain, took us a day or so to pick it back up. Anyway," he sighed continuing, still astounded by the mess in the street, "Looks like they turned on each other and one was chased by two. Found the two dead, so we figure the one who got away with the loot came here."

Penny was listening intently, curious about how this would play out. Having this new perspective. She knew Ash Roberts to be a seasoned investigator and tracker, but a single word jumped out at her.

"Loot? What loot?"

"The cashbox," Bragstone said. Flatly and without explanation.

"Indeed!" Ash Roberts said, in congratulatory tone. He noticed the U. S. Marshal badge on the man's lapel and shook his head apologizing. Penny noticed this too.

"Ash Roberts, this Marshal August Bragstone. Out of Kentucky." She said introducing him.

They shook hands.

Ash looked at the man curiously and then looked back to Penny. Then back to the other marshal.

"What's the name again, son? I'm getting old and been around too many guns," he said with a chuckle.

"August Bragstone," the other marshal said.

"Cashbox?" Penny reiterated, looking between the two marshals. The two went on ignoring her.

"Oh right, right. I've heard the name. And your wife's name! How is the fine Olivia?" he asked beaming with a smile. "Penny, rumor has it this man's wife would make you a pie that'd make you swear allegiance to Jeff Davis!" he laughed.

"Is that so?" Penny asked, imitating a smile. "You didn't mention a wife. Or a cashbox…"

Bragstone smiled and kicked some dirt, "She's fine. Just fine. Sent a letter a few days ago. She's anxious to have me home," he said returning the other marshals smile. Ignoring the sheriff still.

Ash laughed along for a moment and suddenly the smile fled his face. He stared cold at the other marshal. Penny tapered off of her fake smile seeing how serious Ash had gotten. She wasn't sure she had ever seen the man this furrowed. She looked between the two marshals wondering what she missed.

"Ophelia," Ash said, taking the cigar from his mouth. His other hand now dangling closer to his gun.

"What say?" Bragstone asked, still not letting go of his smirk, but noticed Ash's hand moving slowly to his gun.

"August Bragstone's wife," he explained. "Her name is Ophelia. And that women can't cook for shit. And Auggie Bragstone's been dead for two months. Disappeared while tracking a man named Dade. They found his body half eagen by wolves. I was a pall bearer at his funeral."

The imposter sighed heavily and shrugged. He let a moment go by as the sheriff put all the pieces together. He chuckled to himself and clicked his tongue in his cheek, "Almost made it," he said looking up at the marshal.

In a flash, he spun and took Penny by the arm, the wounded arm, and turned her about to put her between himself and the marshal Roberts. In the same fluid motion, he produced a large bowie knife and put its razor edge against Penny's throat.

He was out of bullets and his horse was dead. Had he any rounds left, he would have shot Penny dead right then and there, killed the marshal, the deputy and went after the drifter.

To torture him until he gave up the location of the cashbox.

The sheriff struggled, but her shot arm sent ripples of pain through her. Especially when her captor put his finger in the wound hole to make her more cooperative.

"William Dade, I presume?" the sheriff said through gritted teeth.

"The very same, sheriff," Dade said acknowledging his true name. "Now here's what's going to happen…"

Marshal Ash Roberts held perfectly still.

Jonah walked through town slowly, and blotting his face with a wet clean rag. He felt a few of the scatter shots still in his face, but all in all his head was still in tact.

His arm however was torn to pieces and missing a finger.

He chuckled at himself, letting an old, *old,* woman get the drop on him like that. And as best he could figure that dog wasn't much younger than her.

Jokingly he hoped to himself that the man with the eyepatch wouldn't tell anyone.

Smiling at himself, he came around the corner of the distillery and saw Bragstone holding a large blade to sheriff Penny's throat.

"Ah! Just in time!" Dade said, resetting his grip on Penny's throat and arm.

She cried out in pain.

"What the hell did I miss?" he asked, holding his hands up. The rifle with one shot left was uselessly slung over his shoulder.

Another marshal standing across the way, also frozen in fear that Penny's throat would be cut, said from the corner of his mouth, "That's William Dade, wanted for killing a U. S. Marshal and God-knows how many others."

Jonah looked from the marshal to Dade.

He locked eyes with the man he knew as marshal Bragstone. A man who was actually the very man he accused him of being!

"Zachariah Freeman," Penny said, her wound causing her to almost scream it out.

"What's that you said, beautiful?" Dade said in her ear. He used his blade to flick the top button off her shirt.

"You killed Zachariah!" she said, crying out in sorrow and physical pain.

For a moment Dade looked to the other two men for an explanation. But when Jonah motioned out toward where Zach's cabin was, the imposter gathered it up.

"Oh! The big black oak tree out in the woods?" he asked incredulously. "Hell, honey, that was pretty much just fun chopping that tree down. Never did find that cashbox though. Big blackie didn't know where it was," he laughed. "Did find that gold chunk however! And when you sapped the drifter I slipped it into his pocket, making him my man and set to take the fall. It was all nice and neat until my horse was shot and this badged pile of shit showed up."

Jonah took a step forward willing to risk Penny getting slashed. He twirled the rifle from his shoulder and brought it up to bare. This man nearly had him hanged. What if the sheriff sent for the judge last night? He could be dead by now.

"No, no, loverboy," he warned drawing a line of blood across her throat. "We're gonna take a walk to the blacksmith cabin, us three, but first," he said motioning toward the sheriff's office "You're gonna drop that gun and then lock up this marshal and his dog in your cell."

Jonah didn't move.

He had one shot and Dade was doing well to keep himself hidden behind the sheriff.

"I said drop the rifle or the last thing this cunny sees is her own blood spraying down the street!" he pressed the blade against her throat even more and the fine edge slipped just a hair into her skin.

Penny froze in fear. She felt the blade coming on. Felt the hot breath of Dade on the back of her neck.

That's when Jonah saw his window.

Penny froze.

The drifter looked into her eyes and she looked into his.

"Im sorry, sheriff…"

"Don't you dare," she said, seeing what was to come.

Dade licked his lips and Jonah began to lower his rifle to the dirt.

BANG!

The shot surprised Dade. And Ash Roberts if he was being honest.

Jonah's bullet went through the shoulder meat of Pennys already wounded arm and struck Dade clean in the heart.

The knife hit the ground in a thud.

Penny fell away, going straight down on her rump, clutching her wound in agony.The first shot stung a little because it was a graze and due to the adrenaline of the gunfight, but the drifters second shot burned like the fire of hell when the bullet hit her collarbone. She looked up at a confused Dade, whose left shirt pocket smoked and coughed blood.

"Hey," Dade said in a last moment of perplexity to the sheriff, *"He shot you!"* His tone was accusatory one, as if he faulted the drifter for breaking the rules. He went into a daze. His gun came out and he pulled the trigger several times but it was no more than a series of clicks.

And William Dade collapsed dead.

Jonah let out a long breath.

It was finished.

He tossed the Henry rifle into the dirt and went over to check on Penny.

"You son of a bitch," she said up to him as he got to her. The sheriff's eyes were starting to lull. "You *did* shoot me."

Jonah laughing and apologizing was the last thing Penny remembered before passing out.

"I'm sure sorry about that sheriff …"

But she had slipped away by then. Ash Roberts came over and lifted Penny into his arms. Michaels got her by the boots. He may have been an older law dog, but he was still strong. They started carrying her off to the Doc's office down the street.

Jonah watched him take her for a moment then turned to the sheriff's office. And standing in the midst of the debris and bloodbath was an unharmed Lacey. Covered in shrapnel and her eye kohl running wild from tears, but she was unharmed.

"You survived," she breathed in relief, seeing him there, mostly in one piece. She smiled wide and stomped down off the porch to fall into his arms.

He held her close.

It was over.

The Battle for New Arbor was over.

Somehow, through all of the gunsmoke and fire and blood, she still smelled like rose water.

He laughed and began walking them off toward the Dragoon, where he believed he still had a room rented…

"You know," she said, "I don't even know your real name. *Jonah* – first or last?" she asked, seeing the irony of it all.

"My first name is Ben," he said. No one had called him that since his mother. If Lacey wanted to call him by his first name, that was fine by him.

"Well, Ben, maybe we should get that arm of yours looked at."

EPILOGUE:

In the early morning, two days later, all had been forgiven by Judge Washburn.

There was a rumor that the magistrate was seen leaving Deward's home the morning after the gun fight. Deward defused this speculation by explaining that Judge Washburn had come to check in on Doc Adlard who was resting in grand comfort of the Deward Estate's Master Bedroom. Or he claimed the Judge was there to discuss wedding plans. Or he was there having Deward sign a statement saying that he witnessed Sheriff Landon deputize Ben Jonah, thus legalizing the killing of the Getty men and William Dade.

Of course, it was all a lie. Later that summer the Judge would order a new Celestial wife and build an addition onto his house.

And later that autumn he would lose the election…to Penny Landon.

Jonah and Lacey, with the help of Errol Brown, were packing a small wagon outside of the Dragoon. The Scotsman wasn't pleased about being deceived for years and losing his famous blind singer, but despite all the losses felt by New Arbor, the air of the town was relief that the corrupt Gettys had finally been wiped clean.

The remaining women and children returned to their various families and the estate went up for sale. No one saw Roger Getty ever again.

Jonah was stuffing the last of the supplies into the back when an almost bashful Deward approached him.

"After the fight, so much was happening, I forgot to return this to you."

Deward handed him back his volcanic pistol.

But Jonah held up his bandaged hand.

"No," he said calmly. "You keep it, U. W. You earned it." Jonah winked.

Deward smiled and nodded, recalling the battle just days before.

They shared a moment of silence then, him and his new friend.

"Will the ringing in my ears ever stop?" Deward asked, looking up at him.

Jonah laughed and asked, "*WHAT?*"

They both laughed then.

His ears did still have a slight ringing in them, but he wasn't too worried about that. His hands shook for the first day, but all those anxious tremors in his stomach and hands seemed to flee him the first time he made love to his darling Perlina.

Errol Brown even laughed at the drifter's joke. The bar owner came over and abrasively took the pistol from Deward's hand and began his way back toward the Dragoon.

"I'll hang it o'er the bar! People'll come fer miles to see the famous Deward Horse Gun!" he said, walking away with it, pleased with his new gimmick to replace the blind singer.

The dwarf watched the red-haired man go, "Ah. My father's legacy is now complete. I shall go down in history as the man who shot a horse."

"It assuredly saved my caboose, your quick thinking," Jonah reasoned.

Deward shrugged. He could accept that – being a hero to the hero.

Who could argue with it?

"Perhaps I should be giving you a shovel…" Deward said, hinting at the cashbox.

But Jonah just shook his head, winked and patted the bag of grain he just put on the wagon.

The dwarf chuckled to himself. He truly didn't care about the money. He was a man of his word and more than pleased to let Jonah take it as a payment for how he helped them. Besides, he could always tell Western Union he never received the delivery, which was true, and place the blame on the Pinkertons and seek compensation in court. He had enough for a lifetime without it anyway. And he had his black queen now…God, how he loved her.

"Where will you go?" Deward asked him, holding out his hand to shake it. Just then Lacey came over to stand beside Jonah. "Home? To drift no more?" the lumber baron asked, hopeful that his friend's demons had all gone away.

Jonah looked into Lacey's eyes for a moment. Searching them as if they were the stars.

He took the lumber baron's hand and at long last, after over a decade of drifting and hiding from himself, he nodded.

It was time to go home.

Jonah never again touched a gun, nor a deck of cards, for the rest of his life.

As the wagon, led by two horses, pulled out of town, sheriff Penny Landon watched from her office porch. With her arm in a sling, she sipped at her coffee and watched the couple go.

The office was almost all patched up and Mattie Simon was given to her on leave from the corral to help with hanging a new door.

Jonah looked back over his shoulder at Penny and they shared a moment. As the couple bounced along, he tipped his hat to the sheriff.

Lacey didn't notice the exchange. She looked ahead and dreamed of the Pacific ocean. And wondered if it would be as blue as Ben described.

The sheriff lifted her tin coffee mug to return the man's salute. Jonah saw it and turned away. He pulled a crooked cigarette from his shirt pocket and put it in the corner of his mouth.

He leaned over and asked Lacey a question the sheriff couldn't hear and Lacey, after patting herself down, shook her head 'no.'

Jonah sighed then, took the cigarette from his mouth and threw it down in the street.

Penny snorted, amused. She suspected he was a good man. She could tell that from the moment she met him.

And she hoped for them both to find their way. To have a better life from then on. Perhaps if they did that, God would forget the first half of their lives and bless the second.

The ache in her arm caused her to wince. She looked around the quiet town and felt a new calm and safety had come over the place.

She spilled out her coffee into the street and decided it was quiet enough to have something a bit stronger for the incredible pain.

She took in a deep breath and let it all out at once.

Yes, she believed in her heart that things would be just fine.

"Son of a bitch still shot me though," she said to herself as she stepped through the doorway of her office.

-END

OBITUARY:

Benjamin Miguel Jonah, died yesterday, January 20, 1923 on his 83rd birthday. Exactly one month after his beloved Lacey-Grace. He was at home and surrounded by friends and family. He and his wife lived and found success in Northern California as owners of the Deward & Jonah Fruit Co.

He is survived by their daughter Penny, son Benjamin Jr. and six grandchildren.

Benjamin Jr. sang at both of their funerals.

9 781916 954526